All is calm and genteel in the late-Victorian seaside resort of Folkestone until a mermaid washes ashore.

Miss Doris Thalassia Waters insinuates herself into the lives of wealthy holidaymakers and would-be politicians, seducing some and unsettling others. Her presence throws their relationships into disarray and casts doubt on their most deeply held assumptions.

In this lesser-known but brilliant novella, H. G. Wells blends fantasy and satire to explore questions of nature, society, and desire.

THE SEA LADY

ccc *by* ccc

H. G. WELLS

CHRONICLE BOOKS
SAN FRANCISCO

Library of Congress Cataloging-in-Publication Data available.

ISBN 978-1-7972-2621-7

Manufactured in China.

MIX
Paper | Supporting
responsible forestry
FSC
www.fsc.org
FSC® C169962

Design by Kristen Hewitt.
Cover illustration by Jim Tierney.

10 9 8 7 6 5 4 3 2 1

Chronicle books and gifts are available at special quantity discounts to corporations, professional associations, literacy programs, and other organizations. For details and discount information, please contact our premiums department at corporategifts@chroniclebooks.com or at 1-800-759-0190.

Chronicle Books LLC
680 Second Street
San Francisco, California 94107
www.chroniclebooks.com

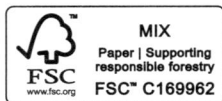

CONTENTS

CHAPTER THE FIRST
THE COMING OF THE SEA LADY

1

Such previous landings of mermaids as have left a record, have all a flavor of doubt. Even the very circumstantial account of that Bruges Sea Lady, who was so clever at fancy work, gives occasion to the skeptic I must confess that I was absolutely incredulous of such things until a year ago. But now, face to face with indisputable facts in my own immediate neighborhood, and with my own second cousin Melville (of Seaton Carew) as the chief witness to the story, I see these old legends in a very different light. Yet so many people concerned themselves with the hushing up of this affair, that, but for my sedulous inquiries I am certain it would have become as doubtful as those older legends in a couple of score of years. Even now to many minds——

The difficulties in the way of the hushing-up process were no doubt exceptionally great in this case, and that they did contrive to do so much, seems to show just how strong are the motives for secrecy in all such cases. There is certainly no remoteness nor obscurity about the scene of these events. They began upon the beach just east of Sandgate Castle, towards Folkestone, and they ended on the beach near Folkestone pier not two miles away. The beginning was in broad daylight on a bright blue day in August and in full sight of the windows of half a dozen houses. At first sight this alone is sufficient to make the popular want of information almost incredible. But of that you may think differently later.

Mrs. Randolph Bunting's two charming daughters were bathing at the time in company with their guest, Miss Mabel Glendower. It is from the latter lady chiefly, and from Mrs. Bunting, that I have pieced together the precise circumstances of the Sea Lady's arrival. From Miss Glendower, the elder of two Glendower girls, for all that she is a principal in almost all that follows, I have obtained, and have sought to obtain, no information whatever. There is the question of the lady's feelings—and in this case I gather they are of a peculiarly complex sort. Quite naturally they would be. At any rate, the natural ruthlessness of the literary calling has failed me. I have not ventured to touch them. . . .

The villa residences to the east of Sandgate Castle, you must understand, are particularly lucky in having gardens that run right down to the beach. There is no intervening esplanade or road or path such as cuts off ninety-nine out of the hundred of houses that face the sea. As you look down on them from the western end of the Leas, you see them crowding the very margin. And as a great number of high groins stand out from the shore along this piece of coast, the beach is practically cut off and made private except at very low water, when people can get around the ends of the groins. These houses are consequently highly desirable during the bathing season, and it is the custom of many of their occupiers to let them furnished during the summer to persons of fashion and affluence.

The Randolph Buntings were such persons—indisputably. It is true of course that they were not Aristocrats, or indeed what an unpaid herald would freely call "gentle." They had no right to any sort of arms. But then, as Mrs. Bunting would sometimes remark, they made no pretense of that sort; they were quite free (as indeed everybody is nowadays) from snobbery. They were simple homely Buntings—Randolph Buntings—"good people" as the saying is—of a widely diffused Hampshire stock addicted to brewing, and whether a suitably remunerated herald could or could not have proved them "gentle" there can be no doubt that Mrs. Bunting was quite justified in taking in the *Gentlewoman*, and that Mr. Bunting and Fred were sedulous gentlemen, and that all their ways and thoughts were delicate and nice. And they had staying with them the two Miss Glendowers, to whom Mrs. Bunting had been something of a mother, ever since Mrs. Glendower's death.

The two Miss Glendowers were half sisters, and gentle beyond dispute, a county family race that had only for a generation stooped to trade, and risen at once Antæus-like, refreshed and enriched. The elder, Adeline, was the rich one—the heiress, with the commercial blood in her veins. She was really very rich, and she had dark hair and gray eyes and serious views, and when her father died, which he did a little before her step-mother, she had only the later portion of her later youth left to her. She was nearly seven-and-twenty. She had sacrificed her earlier youth to her father's infirmity of temper in a way that had always reminded her of the girlhood of Elizabeth Barrett Browning. But after his departure for a sphere where his temper has no doubt a wider scope—for what is this world for if it is not for the Formation of Character?—she had come out strongly. It became evident she had always had a mind, and a very active and capable one, an accumulated fund of energy and much ambition. She had bloomed into a clear and critical socialism, and she had blossomed at public meetings; and now she was engaged to that really very brilliant and promising but rather extravagant and romantic person, Harry Chatteris, the nephew of an earl and the hero of a scandal, and quite a possible Liberal candidate for the Hythe division of Kent. At least this last matter was under discussion and he was about, and Miss Glendower liked to feel she was supporting him by being about too, and that was chiefly why the Buntings had taken a house in Sandgate for the summer. Sometimes he would come and stay a night or so with them, sometimes he would be off upon affairs, for he was known to be a very versatile, brilliant, first-class political young man—and Hythe very lucky to have a bid for him, all things considered. And Fred Bunting was engaged to Miss Glendower's less distinguished, much less wealthy, seventeen-year-old and possibly altogether more ordinary half sister, Mabel Glendower, who had discerned long since when they were at school together that it wasn't any good trying to be clear when Adeline was about.

The Buntings did not bathe "mixed," a thing indeed that was still only very doubtfully decent in 1898, but Mr. Randolph Bunting and his son Fred came down to the beach with them frankly instead of hiding away or going for a walk according to the older fashion. (This, notwithstanding that Miss Mabel Glendower, Fred's *fiancée* to boot, was of the bathing party.) They formed a little procession down under the evergreen oaks in the garden and down the ladder and so to the sea's margin.

Mrs. Bunting went first, looking as it were for Peeping Tom with her glasses, and Miss Glendower, who never bathed because it made her feel undignified, went with her—wearing one of those simple, costly "art" morning costumes Socialists affect. Behind this protecting van came, one by one, the three girls, in their beautiful Parisian bathing dresses and headdresses—though these were of course completely muffled up in huge hooded gowns of toweling—and wearing of course stockings and shoes—they bathed in stockings and shoes. Then came Mrs. Bunting's maid and the second housemaid and the maid the Glendower girls had brought, carrying towels, and then at a little interval the two men carrying ropes and things. (Mrs. Bunting always put a rope around each of her daughters before ever they put a foot in the water and held it until they were safely out again. But Mabel Glendower would not have a rope.)

Where the garden ends and the beach begins Miss Glendower turned aside and sat down on the green iron seat under the evergreen oak, and having found her place in *Sir George Tressady*—a book of which she was naturally enough at that time inordinately fond—sat watching the others go on down the beach. There they were a very bright and very pleasant group of prosperous animated people upon the sunlit beach, and beyond them in streaks of gray and purple, and altogether calm save for a pattern of dainty little wavelets, was that ancient mother of surprises, the Sea.

As soon as they reached the high-water mark where it is no longer indecent to be clad merely in a bathing dress, each of the young ladies handed her attendant her wrap, and after a little fun and laughter Mrs. Bunting looked carefully to see if there were any jelly fish, and then they went in. And after a minute or so, it seems Betty, the elder Miss Bunting, stopped splashing and looked, and then they all looked, and there, about thirty yards away was the Sea Lady's head, as if she were swimming back to land.

Naturally they concluded that she must be a neighbor from one of the adjacent houses. They were a little surprised not to have noticed her going down into the water, but beyond that her apparition had no shadow of wonder for them. They made the furtive penetrating observations usual in such cases. They could see that she was swimming very gracefully and that she had a lovely face and very beautiful arms, but they could not see her wonderful golden hair because all that was hidden in a fashionable Phrygian bathing cap, picked up—as she afterwards admitted to my second cousin—some nights before upon a Norman *plage*. Nor could they see her lovely shoulders because of the red costume she wore.

They were just on the point of feeling their inspection had reached the limit of really nice manners and Mabel was pretending to go on splashing again and saying to Betty, "She's wearing a red dress. I wish I could see—" when something very terrible happened.

The swimmer gave a queer sort of flop in the water, threw up her arms and—vanished!

It was the sort of thing that seems for an instant to freeze everybody, just one of those things that everyone has read of and imagined and very few people have seen.

For a space no one did anything. One, two, three seconds passed and then for an instant a bare arm flashed in the air and vanished again.

Mabel tells me she was quite paralyzed with horror, she did nothing all the time, but the two Miss Buntings, recovering a little, screamed out, "Oh, she's drowning!" and hastened to get out of the sea at once, a proceeding accelerated by Mrs. Bunting, who with great presence of mind pulled at the ropes with all her weight and turned about and continued to pull long after they were many yards from the water's edge and indeed cowering in a heap at the foot of the sea wall. Miss Glendower became aware of a crisis and descended the steps, *Sir George Tressady* in one hand and the other shading her eyes, crying in her clear resolute voice, "She must be saved!" The maids of course were screaming—as became them—but the two men appear to have acted with the greatest presence of mind. "Fred, Nexdoors ledder!" said Mr. Randolph Bunting—for the next-door neighbor instead of having convenient stone steps had a high wall and a long wooden ladder, and it had often been pointed out by Mr. Bunting if ever an accident should happen to anyone there was *that!* In a moment it seems they had both flung off jacket and vest, collar, tie and shoes, and were running the neighbor's ladder out into the water.

"Where did she go, Ded?" said Fred.

"Right out hea!" said Mr. Bunting, and to confirm his word there flashed again an arm and "something dark"—something which in the light of all that subsequently happened I am inclined to suppose was an unintentional exposure of the Lady's tail.

Neither of the two gentlemen are expert swimmers—indeed so far as I can gather, Mr. Bunting in the excitement of the occasion forgot almost everything he had ever known of swimming—but they waded out valiantly one on each side of the ladder, thrust it out before them and committed themselves to the deep, in a manner casting no discredit upon our nation and race.

Yet on the whole I think it is a matter for general congratulation that they were not engaged in the rescue of a genuinely drowning person. At the time of my inquiries whatever soreness of argument that may once have obtained between them had passed, and it is fairly clear that while Fred Bunting was engaged in swimming hard against the long side of the ladder and so causing it to rotate slowly on its axis, Mr. Bunting had already swallowed a very considerable amount of sea-water and was kicking Fred in the chest with aimless vigor. This he did, as he explains, "to get my legs down, you know. Something about that ladder, you know, and they *would* go up!"

And then quite unexpectedly the Sea Lady appeared beside them. One lovely arm supported Mr. Bunting about the waist and the other was over the ladder. She did not appear at all pale or frightened or out of breath, Fred told me when I cross-examined him, though at the time he was too violently excited to note a detail of that sort. Indeed she smiled and spoke in an easy pleasant voice.

"Cramp," she said, "I have cramp." Both the men were convinced of that.

Mr. Bunting was on the point of telling her to hold tight and she would be quite safe, when a little wave went almost entirely into his mouth and reduced him to wild splutterings.

"*We'll* get you in," said Fred, or something of that sort, and so they all hung, bobbing in the water to the tune of Mr. Bunting's trouble.

They seem to have rocked so for some time. Fred says the Sea Lady looked calm but a little puzzled and that she seemed to measure the distance shoreward. "You *mean* to save me?" she asked him.

He was trying to think what could be done before his father drowned. "We're saving you now," he said.

"You'll take me ashore?"

As she seemed so cool he thought he would explain his plan of operations, "Trying to get—end of ladder—kick with my legs. Only a few yards out of our depth—if we could only——"

"Minute—get my breath—moufu' sea-water," said Mr. Bunting. *Splash!* wuff! . . .

And then it seemed to Fred that a little miracle happened. There was a swirl of the water like the swirl about a screw propeller, and he gripped the Sea Lady and the ladder just in time, as it seemed to him, to prevent his being washed far out into the Channel. His father vanished from his sight with an expression of astonishment just forming on his face and reappeared beside him, so far as back and legs are concerned, holding on to the ladder with a sort of death grip. And then behold! They had shifted a dozen yards inshore, and they were in less than five feet of water and Fred could feel the ground.

At its touch his amazement and dismay immediately gave way to the purest heroism. He thrust ladder and Sea Lady before him, abandoned the ladder and his now quite disordered parent, caught her tightly in his arms, and bore her up out of the water. The young ladies cried "Saved!" the maids cried "Saved!" Distant voices echoed "Saved, Hooray!" Everybody in fact cried "Saved!" except Mrs. Bunting, who was, she says, under the impression that Mr. Bunting was in a fit, and Mr. Bunting, who seems to have been under an impression that all those laws of nature by which, under Providence, we are permitted to float and swim, were in suspense and that the best thing to do was to kick very hard and fast until the end should come. But in a dozen seconds or so his head was up again and his feet were on the ground and he was making whale and walrus noises, and noises like a horse and like an angry cat and like sawing, and was wiping the water from his eyes; and Mrs. Bunting (except that now and then she really *had* to turn and say "*Ran*dolph!") could give her attention to the beautiful burthen that clung about her son.

And it is a curious thing that the Sea Lady was at least a minute out of the water before anyone discovered that she was in any way different from—other ladies. I suppose they were all crowding close to her and looking at her beautiful face, or perhaps they imagined that she was wearing some indiscreet but novel form of dark riding habit or something of that sort. Anyhow not one of them noticed it, although it must have been before their eyes as plain as day. Certainly it must have blended with the costume. And there they stood, imagining that Fred had rescued a lovely lady of indisputable fashion, who had been bathing from some neighboring house, and wondering why on earth there was nobody on the beach to claim her. And she clung to Fred and, as Miss Mabel Glendower subsequently remarked in the course of conversation with him, Fred clung to her.

"I had cramp," said the Sea Lady, with her lips against Fred's cheek and one eye on Mrs. Bunting. "I am sure it was cramp. . . . I've got it still."

"I don't see anybody—" began Mrs. Bunting.

"Please carry me in," said the Sea Lady, closing her eyes as if she were ill—though her cheek was flushed and warm. "Carry me in."

"Where?" gasped Fred.

"Carry me into the house," she whispered to him.

"Which house?"

Mrs. Bunting came nearer.

"*Your* house," said the Sea Lady, and shut her eyes for good and became oblivious to all further remarks.

"She— But I don't understand—" said Mrs. Bunting, addressing everybody. . . .

And then it was they saw it. Nettie, the younger Miss Bunting, saw it first. She pointed, she says, before she could find words to speak. Then they all saw it! Miss Glendower, I believe, was the person who was last to see it. At any rate it would have been like her if she had been.

"Mother," said Nettie, giving words to the general horror. "*Mother!* She has a *tail!*"

And then the three maids and Mabel Glendower screamed one after the other. "Look!" they cried. "A tail!"

"Of all—" said Mrs. Bunting, and words failed her.

"*Oh!*" said Miss Glendower, and put her hand to her heart.

And then one of the maids gave it a name. "It's a mermaid!" screamed the maid, and then everyone screamed, "It's a mermaid."

Except the mermaid herself; she remained quite passive, pretending to be insensible partly on Fred's shoulder and altogether in his arms.

II

That, you know, is the tableau so far as I have been able to piece it together again. You must imagine this little knot of people upon the beach, and Mr. Bunting, I figure, a little apart, just wading out of the water and very wet and incredulous and half drowned. And the neighbor's ladder was drifting quietly out to sea.

Of course it was one of those positions that have an air of being conspicuous.

Indeed it was conspicuous. It was some way below high water and the group stood out perhaps thirty yards down the beach. Nobody, as Mrs. Bunting told my cousin Melville, knew a bit *what* to do and they all had even an exaggerated share of the national hatred of being seen in a puzzle. The mermaid seemed content to remain a beautiful problem clinging to Fred, and by all accounts she was a reasonable burthen for a man. It seems that the very large family of people who were stopping at the house called Koot Hoomi had appeared in force, and they were all staring and gesticulating. They were just the sort of people the Buntings did not want to know—tradespeople very probably. Presently one of the men—the particularly vulgar man who used to shoot at the gulls—began putting down their ladder as if he intended to offer advice, and Mrs. Bunting also became aware of the black glare of the field glasses of a still more horrid man to the west.

Moreover the popular author who lived next door, an irascible dark square-headed little man in spectacles, suddenly turned up and began bawling from his inaccessible wall top something foolish about his ladder. Nobody thought of his silly ladder or took any trouble about it, naturally. He was quite stupidly excited. To judge by his tone and gestures he was using dreadful language and seemed disposed every moment to jump down to the beach and come to them.

And then to crown the situation, over the westward groin appeared Low Excursionists!

First of all their heads came, and then their remarks. Then they began to clamber the breakwater with joyful shouts.

"Pip, Pip," said the Low Excursionists as they climbed—it was the year of "pip, pip"—and, "What HO she bumps!" and then less generally, "What's up 'ere?"

And the voices of other Low Excursionists still invisible answered, 'Pip, Pip.'

It was evidently a large party.

"Anything wrong?" shouted one of the Low Excursionists at a venture.

"My *dear!*" said Mrs. Bunting to Mabel, "what *are* we to do?" And in her description of the affair to my cousin Melville she used always to make that the *clou* of the story. "My DEAR! What ARE we to do?"

I believe that in her desperation she even glanced at the water. But of course to have put the mermaid back then would have involved the most terrible explanations. . . .

It was evident there was only one thing to be done. Mrs. Bunting said as much. "The only thing," said she, "is to carry her indoors."

And carry her indoors they did! . . .

One can figure the little procession. In front Fred, wet and astonished but still clinging and clung to, and altogether too out of breath for words. And in his arms the Sea Lady. She had a beautiful figure, I understand, until that horrible tail began (and the fin of it, Mrs. Bunting told my cousin in a whispered confidence, went up and down and with pointed corners for all the world like a mackerel's). It flopped and dripped along the path—I imagine. She was wearing a very nice and very long-skirted dress of red material trimmed with coarse white lace, and she had, Mabel told me, a *gilet*, though that would scarcely show as they went up the garden. And that Phrygian cap hid all her golden hair and showed the white, low, level forehead over her sea-blue eyes. From all that followed, I imagine her at the moment scanning the veranda and windows of the house with a certain eagerness of scrutiny.

Behind this staggering group of two I believe Mrs. Bunting came. Then Mr. Bunting. Dreadfully wet and broken down Mr. Bunting must have been by then, and from one or two things I have noticed since, I can't help imagining him as pursuing his wife with, "Of course, my dear, *I* couldn't tell, you know!"

And then, in a dismayed yet curious bunch, the girls in their wraps of toweling and the maids carrying the ropes and things and, as if inadvertently, as became them, most of Mr. and Fred Bunting's clothes.

And then Miss Glendower, for once at least in no sort of pose whatever, clutching *Sir George Tressady* and perplexed and disturbed beyond measure.

And then, as it were pursuing them all, "Pip, pip," and the hat and raised eyebrows of a Low Excursionist still anxious to know "What's up?" from the garden end.

So it was, or at least in some such way, and to the accompaniment of the wildest ravings about some ladder or other heard all too distinctly over the garden wall—("Overdressed Snobbs take my *rare old English adjective* ladder . . . !")—that they carried the Sea Lady (who appeared serenely insensible to everything) up through the house and laid her down upon the couch in Mrs. Bunting's room.

And just as Miss Glendower was suggesting that the very best thing they could do would be to send for a doctor, the Sea Lady with a beautiful naturalness sighed and came to.

SOME FIRST IMPRESSIONS

I

There with as much verisimilitude as I can give it, is how the Folkestone mermaid really came to land. There can be no doubt that the whole affair was a deliberately planned intrusion upon her part. She never had cramp, she couldn't have cramp, and as for drowning, nobody was near drowning for a moment except Mr. Bunting, whose valuable life she very nearly sacrificed at the outset of her adventure. And her next proceeding was to demand an interview with Mrs. Bunting and to presume upon her youthful and glowing appearance to gain the support, sympathy and assistance of that good-hearted lady (who as a matter of fact was a thing of yesterday, a mere chicken in comparison with her own immemorial years) in her extraordinary raid upon Humanity.

Her treatment of Mrs. Bunting would be incredible if we did not know that, in spite of many disadvantages, the Sea Lady was an extremely well read person. She admitted as much in several later conversations with my cousin Melville. For a time there was a friendly intimacy—so Melville always preferred to present it—between these two, and my cousin, who has a fairly considerable amount of curiosity, learned many very interesting details about the life "out there" or "down there"—for the Sea Lady used either expression. At first the Sea Lady was exceedingly reticent under the gentle insistence of his curiosity, but after a time, I gather, she gave way to bursts of cheerful confidence. "It is clear," says my cousin, "that the old ideas of the submarine life as a sort of perpetual game of 'who-hoop' through groves of coral, diversified by moonlight hair-combings on rocky strands, need very extensive modification." In this matter of literature, for example, they have practically all that we have, and unlimited leisure to read it in. Melville is very insistent upon and rather envious of that unlimited leisure. A picture of a mermaid swinging in a hammock of woven seaweed, with what bishops call a "latter-day" novel in one hand and a sixteen candle-power phosphorescent fish in the other, may jar upon one's preconceptions, but it is certainly far more in accordance with the picture of the abyss she printed on his mind. Everywhere Change works her will on things. Everywhere, and even among the immortals, Modernity spreads. Even on Olympus I suppose there is a Progressive party and a new Phaeton agitating to supersede the horses of his father by some solar motor of his own. I suggested as much to Melville and he said "Horrible! Horrible!" and stared hard at my study fire. Dear old Melville! She gave him no end of facts about Deep Sea Reading.

Of course they do not print books "out there," for the printer's ink under water would not so much run as fly—she made that very plain; but in one way or another nearly the whole of terrestrial literature, says Melville, has come to them. "We know," she said. They form indeed a distinct reading public, and additions to their vast submerged library that circulates forever with the tides, are now pretty systematically sought. The sources are various and in some cases a little odd. Many books have been found in sunken ships. "Indeed!" said Melville. There is always a dropping and blowing overboard of novels and magazines from most passenger-carrying vessels—sometimes, but these are not as a rule valuable additions—a deliberate shying overboard. But sometimes books of an exceptional sort are thrown over when they are quite finished. (Melville is a dainty irritable reader and no doubt he understood that.) From the sea beaches of holiday resorts, moreover, the lighter sorts of literature are occasionally getting blown out to sea. And so soon as the Booms of our great Popular Novelists are over, Melville assured me, the libraries find it convenient to cast such surplus copies of their current works as the hospitals and prisons cannot take, below high-water mark.

"That's not generally known," said I.

"*They* know it," said Melville.

In other ways the beaches yield. Young couples who "begin to sit heapy," the Sea Lady told my cousin, as often as not will leave excellent modern fiction behind them, when at last they return to their proper place. There is a particularly fine collection of English work, it seems, in the deep water of the English Channel; practically the whole of the Tauchnitz Library is there, thrown overboard at the last moment by conscientious or timid travelers returning from the continent, and there was for a time a similar source of supply of American reprints in the Mersey, but that has fallen off in recent years. And the Deep Sea Mission for Fishermen has now for some years been raining down tracts and giving a particularly elevated tone of thought to the extensive shallows of the North Sea. The Sea Lady was very precise on these points.

When one considers the conditions of its accumulation, one is not surprised to hear that the element of fiction is as dominant in this Deep Sea Library as it is upon the counters of Messrs. Mudie; but my cousin learned that the various illustrated magazines, and particularly the fashion papers, are valued even more highly than novels, are looked for far more eagerly and perused with envious emotion. Indeed on that point my cousin got a sudden glimpse of one of the motives that had brought this daring young lady into the air. He made some sort of suggestion. "We should have taken to dressing long ago," she said, and added, with a vague quality of laughter in her tone, "it isn't that we're unfeminine, Mr. Melville. Only—as I was explaining to Mrs. Bunting, one must consider one's circumstances—how *can* one *hope* to keep anything nice under water? Imagine lace!"

"Soaked!" said my cousin Melville.

"Drenched!" said the Sea Lady.

"Ruined!" said my cousin Melville.

"And then you know," said the Sea Lady very gravely, "one's hair!"

"Of course," said Melville. "Why!—you can never get it *dry!*"

"That's precisely it," said she.

My cousin Melville had a new light on an old topic. "And that's why—in the old time——?"

"Exactly!" she cried, "exactly! Before there were so many Excursionists and sailors and Low People about, one came out, one sat and brushed it in the sun. And then of course it really *was* possible to do it up. But now——"

She made a petulant gesture and looked gravely at Melville, biting her lip the while. My cousin made a sympathetic noise. "The horrid modern spirit," he said—almost automatically. . . .

But though fiction and fashion appear to be so regrettably dominant in the nourishment of the mer-mind, it must not be supposed that the most serious side of our reading never reaches the bottom of the sea. There was, for example, a case quite recently, the Sea Lady said, of the captain of a sailing ship whose mind had become unhinged by the huckstering uproar of the *Times* and *Daily Mail*, and who had not only bought a second-hand copy of the *Times* reprint of the Encyclopædia Britannica, but also that dense collection of literary snacks and samples, that All-Literature Sausage which has been compressed under the weighty editing of Doctor Richard Garnett. It has long been notorious that even the greatest minds of the past were far too copious and confusing in their—as the word goes—lubrications. Doctor Garnett, it is alleged, has seized the gist and presented it so compactly that almost any business man now may take hold of it without hindrance to his more serious occupations. The unfortunate and misguided seaman seems to have carried the entire collection aboard with him, with the pretty evident intention of coming to land in Sydney the wisest man alive—a Hindoo-minded thing to do. The result might have been anticipated. The mass shifted in the night, threw the whole weight of the science of the middle nineteenth century and the literature of all time, in a virulently concentrated state, on one side of his little vessel and capsized it instantly. . . .

The ship, the Sea Lady said, dropped into the abyss as if it were loaded with lead, and its crew and other movables did not follow it down until much later in the day. The captain was the first to arrive, said the Sea Lady, and it is a curious fact, due probably to some preliminary dippings into his purchase, that he came head first, instead of feet down and limbs expanded in the customary way. . . .

However, such exceptional windfalls avail little against the rain of light literature that is constantly going on. The novel and the newspaper remain the world's reading even at the bottom of the sea. As subsequent events would seem to show, it must have been from the common latter-day novel and the newspaper that the Sea Lady derived her ideas of human life and sentiment and the inspiration of her visit. And if at times she seemed to underestimate the nobler tendencies of the human spirit, if at times she seemed disposed to treat Adeline Glendower and many of the deeper things of life with a certain skeptical levity, if she did at last indisputably subordinate reason and right feeling to passion, it is only just to her, and to those deeper issues, that we should ascribe her aberrations to their proper cause. . . .

II

My cousin Melville, I was saying, did at one time or another get a vague, a very vague conception of what that deep-sea world was like. But whether his conception has any quality of truth in it is more than I dare say. He gives me an impression of a very strange world indeed, a green luminous fluidity in which these beings float, a world lit by great shining monsters that drift athwart it, and by waving forests of nebulous luminosity amidst which the little fishes drift like netted stars. It is a world with neither sitting, nor standing, nor going, nor coming, through which its inhabitants float and drift as one floats and drifts in dreams. And the way they live there! "My dear man!" said Melville, "it must be like a painted ceiling! . . ."

I do not even feel certain that it is in the sea particularly that this world of the Sea Lady is to be found. But about those saturated books and drowned scraps of paper, you say? Things are not always what they seem, and she told him all of that, we must reflect, one laughing afternoon.

She could appear, at times, he says, as real as you or I, and again came mystery all about her. There were times when it seemed to him you might have hurt her or killed her as you can hurt and kill anyone—with a penknife for example—and there were times when it seemed to him you could have destroyed the whole material universe and left her smiling still. But of this ambiguous element in the lady, more is to be told later. There are wider seas than ever keel sailed upon, and deeps that no lead of human casting will ever plumb. When it is all summed up, I have to admit, I do not know, I cannot tell. I fall back upon Melville and my poor array of collected facts. At first there was amazingly little strangeness about her for any who had to deal with her. There she was, palpably solid and material, a lady out of the sea.

This modern world is a world where the wonderful is utterly commonplace. We are bred to show a quiet freedom from amazement, and why should we boggle at material Mermaids, with Dewars solidifying all sorts of impalpable things and Marconi waves spreading everywhere? To the Buntings she was as matter of fact, as much a matter of authentic and reasonable motives and of sound solid sentimentality, as everything else in the Bunting world. So she was for them in the beginning, and so up to this day with them her memory remains.

III

The way in which the Sea Lady talked to Mrs. Bunting on that memorable morning, when she lay all wet and still visibly fishy on the couch in Mrs. Bunting's dressing-room, I am also able to give with some little fulness, because Mrs. Bunting repeated it all several times, acting the more dramatic speeches in it, to my cousin Melville in several of those good long talks that both of them in those happy days—and particularly Mrs. Bunting—always enjoyed so much. And with her very first speech, it seems, the Sea Lady took her line straight to Mrs. Bunting's generous managing heart. She sat up on the couch, drew the antimacassar modestly over her deformity, and sometimes looking sweetly down and sometimes openly and trustfully into Mrs. Bunting's face, and speaking in a soft clear grammatical manner that stamped her at once as no mere mermaid but a finished fine Sea Lady, she "made a clean breast of it," as Mrs. Bunting said, and "fully and frankly" placed herself in Mrs. Bunting's hands.

"Mrs. Bunting," said Mrs. Bunting to my cousin Melville, in a dramatic rendering of the Sea Lady's manner, "do permit me to apologize for this intrusion, for I know it *is* an intrusion. But indeed it has almost been *forced* upon me, and if you will only listen to my story, Mrs. Bunting, I think you will find—well, if not a complete excuse for me—for I can understand how exacting your standards must be—at any rate *some* excuse for what I have done—for what I *must* call, Mrs. Bunting, my deceitful conduct towards you. Deceitful it was, Mrs. Bunting, for I never had cramp— But then, Mrs. Bunting"—and here Mrs. Bunting would insert a long impressive pause—"I never had a mother!"

"And then and there," said Mrs. Bunting, when she told the story to my cousin Melville, "the poor child burst into tears and confessed she had been born ages and ages ago in some dreadful miraculous way in some terrible place near Cyprus, and had no more right to a surname—Well, *there*—!" said Mrs. Bunting, telling the story to my cousin Melville and making the characteristic gesture with which she always passed over and disowned any indelicacy to which her thoughts might have tended. "And all the while speaking with such a nice accent and moving in such a ladylike way!"

"Of course," said my cousin Melville, "there are classes of people in whom one excuses— One must weigh——"

"Precisely," said Mrs. Bunting. "And you see it seems she deliberately chose *me* as the very sort of person she had always wanted to appeal to. It wasn't as if she came to us haphazard—she picked us out. She had been swimming round the coast watching people day after day, she said, for quite a long time, and she said when she saw my face, watching the girls bathe—you know how funny girls are," said Mrs. Bunting, with a little deprecatory laugh, and all the while with a moisture of emotion in her kindly eyes. "She took quite a violent fancy to me from the very first."

"I can *quite* believe *that*, at any rate," said my cousin Melville with unction. I know he did, although he always leaves it out of the story when he tells it to me. But then he forgets that I have had the occasional privilege of making a third party in these good long talks.

"You know it's most extraordinary and exactly like the German story," said Mrs. Bunting. "Oom—what is it?"

"Undine?"

"Exactly—yes. And it really seems these poor creatures are Immortal, Mr. Melville—at least within limits—creatures born of the elements and resolved into the elements again—and just as it is in the story—there's always a something—they have no Souls! No Souls at all! Nothing! And the poor child feels it. She feels it dreadfully. But in order to *get* souls, Mr. Melville, you know they have to come into the world of men. At least so they believe down there. And so she has come to Folkestone. To get a soul. Of course that's her great object, Mr. Melville, but she's not at all fanatical or silly about it. Any more than *we* are. Of course *we*—people who feel deeply——"

"Of course," said my cousin Melville, with, I know, a momentary expression of profound gravity, drooping eyelids and a hushed voice. For my cousin does a good deal with his soul, one way and another.

"And she feels that if she comes to earth at all," said Mrs. Bunting, "she *must* come among *nice* people and in a nice way. One can understand her feeling like that. But imagine her difficulties! To be a mere cause of public excitement, and silly paragraphs in the silly season, to be made a sort of show of, in fact—she doesn't want *any* of it," added Mrs. Bunting, with the emphasis of both hands.

"What *does* she want?" asked my cousin Melville.

"She wants to be treated exactly like a human being, to *be* a human being, just like you or me. And she asks to stay with us, to be one of our family, and to learn how we live. She has asked me to advise her what books to read that are really nice, and where she can get a dress-maker, and how she can find a clergyman to sit under who would really be likely to understand her case, and everything. She wants me to advise her about it all. She wants to put herself altogether in my hands. And she asked it all so nicely and sweetly. She wants me to advise her about it all."

"Um," said my cousin Melville.

"You should have heard her!" cried Mrs. Bunting.

"Practically it's another daughter," he reflected.

"Yes," said Mrs. Bunting, "and even that did not frighten me. She admitted as much."

"Still——"

He took a step.

"She has means?" he inquired abruptly.

"Ample. She told me there was a box. She said it was moored at the end of a groin, and accordingly dear Randolph watched all through luncheon, and afterwards, when they could wade out and reach the end of the rope that tied it, he and Fred pulled it in and helped Fitch and the coachman carry it up. It's a curious little box for a lady to have, well made, of course, but of wood, with a ship painted on the top and the name of 'Tom' cut in it roughly with a knife; but, as she says, leather simply will *not* last down there, and one has to put up with what one can get; and the great thing is it's *full*, perfectly full, of gold coins and things. Yes, gold—and diamonds, Mr. Melville. You know Randolph understands something—Yes, well he says that box—oh! I couldn't tell you *how* much it isn't worth! And all the gold things with just a sort of faint reddy touch. . . . But any-how, she is rich, as well as charming and beautiful. And really you know, Mr. Melville, altogether— Well, I'm going to help her, just as much as ever I can. Practically, she's to be our paying guest. As you know—it's no great secret between *us*—Adeline— Yes. . . . She'll be the same. And I shall bring her out and introduce her to people and so forth. It will be a great help. And for everyone except just a few intimate friends, she is to be just a human being who happens to be an invalid—temporarily an invalid—and we are going to engage a good, trustworthy woman—the sort of woman who isn't astonished at anything, you know—they're a little expensive but they're to be got even nowadays—who will be her maid—and make her dresses, her skirts at any rate—and we shall dress her in long skirts—and throw something over It, you know——"

"Over——?"

"The tail, you know."

My cousin Melville said "Precisely!" with his head and eyebrows. But that was the point that hadn't been clear to him so far, and it took his breath away. Positively—a tail! All sorts of incorrect theories went by the board. Somehow he felt this was a topic not to be too urgently pursued. But he and Mrs. Bunting were old friends.

"And she really has . . . a tail?" he asked.

"Like the tail of a big mackerel," said Mrs. Bunting, and he asked no more.

"It's a most extraordinary situation," he said.

"But what else *could* I do?" asked Mrs. Bunting.

"Of course the thing's a tremendous experiment," said my cousin Melville, and repeated quite inadvertently, "*a tail!*"

Clear and vivid before his eyes, obstructing absolutely the advance of his thoughts, were the shiny clear lines, the oily black, the green and purple and silver, and the easy expansiveness of a mackerel's termination.

"But really, you know," said my cousin Melville, protesting in the name of reason and the nineteenth century—"a tail!"

"I patted it," said Mrs. Bunting.

IV

Certain supplementary aspects of the Sea Lady's first conversation with Mrs. Bunting I got from that lady herself afterwards.

The Sea Lady had made one queer mistake. "Your four charming daughters," she said, "and your two sons."

"My dear!" cried Mrs. Bunting—they had got through their preliminaries by then—"I've only two daughters and one son!"

"The young man who carried—who rescued me?"

"Yes. And the other two girls are friends, you know, visitors who are staying with me. On land one has visitors——"

"I know. So I made a mistake?"

"Oh yes."

"And the other young man?"

"You don't mean Mr. Bunting."

"Who is Mr. Bunting?"

"The other gentleman who——"

"*No!*"

"There was no one——"

"But several mornings ago?"

"Could it have been Mr. Melville? . . . *I* know! You mean Mr. Chatteris! I remember, he came down with us one morning. A tall young man with fair—rather curlyish you might say—hair, wasn't it? And a rather thoughtful face. He was dressed all in white linen and he sat on the beach."

"I fancy he did," said the Sea Lady.

"He's not my son. He's—he's a friend. He's engaged to Adeline, to the elder Miss Glendower. He was stopping here for a night or so. I daresay he'll come again on his way back from Paris. Dear me! Fancy *my* having a son like that!"

The Sea Lady was not quite prompt in replying.

"What a stupid mistake for me to make!" she said slowly; and then with more animation, "Of course, now I think, he's much too old to be your son!"

"Well, he's thirty-two!" said Mrs. Bunting with a smile.

"It's preposterous."

"I won't say *that*."

"But I saw him only at a distance, you know," said the Sea Lady; and then, "And so he is engaged to Miss Glendower? And Miss Glendower——?"

"Is the young lady in the purple robe who——"

"Who carried a book?"

"Yes," said Mrs. Bunting, "that's the one. They've been engaged three months."

"Dear me!" said the Sea Lady. "She seemed— And is he very much in love with her?"

"Of course," said Mrs. Bunting.

"*Very* much?"

"Oh—of *course*. If he wasn't, he wouldn't——"

"Of course," said the Sea Lady thoughtfully.

"And it's such an excellent match in every way. Adeline's just in the very position to help him——"

And Mrs. Bunting it would seem briefly but clearly supplied an indication of the precise position of Mr. Chatteris, not omitting even that he was the nephew of an earl, as indeed why should she omit it?—and the splendid prospects of his alliance with Miss Glendower's plebeian but extensive wealth. The Sea Lady listened gravely. "He is young, he is able, he may still be anything—anything. And she is so earnest, so clever herself—always reading. She even reads Blue Books—government Blue Books I mean—dreadful statistical schedulely things. And the condition of the poor and all those things. She knows more about the condition of the poor than any one I've ever met; what they earn and what they eat, and how many of them live in a room. So dreadfully crowded, you know—perfectly shocking. . . . She is just the helper he needs. So dignified—so capable of giving political parties and influencing people, so earnest! And you know she can talk to workmen and take an interest in trades unions, and in quite astonishing things. *I* always think she's just *Marcella* come to life."

And from that the good lady embarked upon an illustrative but involved anecdote of Miss Glendower's marvelous blue-bookishness. . . .

"He'll come here again soon?" the Sea Lady asked quite carelessly in the midst of it.

The query was carried away and lost in the anecdote, so that later the Sea Lady repeated her question even more carelessly.

But Mrs. Bunting did not know whether the Sea Lady sighed at all or not. She thinks not. She was so busy telling her all about everything that I don't think she troubled very much to see how her information was received.

What mind she had left over from her own discourse was probably centered on the tail.

V

Even to Mrs. Bunting's senses—she is one of those persons who take everything (except of course impertinence or impropriety) quite calmly—it must, I think, have been a little astonishing to find herself sitting in her boudoir, politely taking tea with a real live legendary creature. They were having tea in the boudoir, because of callers, and quite quietly because, in spite of the Sea Lady's smiling assurances, Mrs. Bunting would have it she *must* be tired and unequal to the exertions of social intercourse. "After *such* a journey," said Mrs. Bunting. There were just the three, Adeline Glendower being the third; and Fred and the three other girls, I understand, hung about in a general sort of way up and down the staircase (to the great annoyance of the servants who were thus kept out of it altogether) confirming one another's views of the tail, arguing on the theory of mermaids, revisiting the garden and beach and trying to invent an excuse for seeing the invalid again. They were forbidden to intrude and pledged to secrecy by Mrs. Bunting, and they must have been as altogether unsettled and miserable as young people can be. For a time they played croquet in a half-hearted way, each no doubt with an eye on the boudoir window.

(And as for Mr. Bunting, he was in bed.)

I gather that the three ladies sat and talked as any three ladies all quite resolved to be pleasant to one another would talk. Mrs. Bunting and Miss Glendower were far too well trained in the observances of good society (which is as every one knows, even the best of it now, extremely mixed) to make too searching inquiries into the Sea Lady's status and way of life or precisely where she lived when she was at home, or whom she knew or didn't know. Though in their several ways they wanted to know badly enough. The Sea Lady volunteered no information, contenting herself with an entertaining superficiality of touch and go, in the most ladylike way. She professed herself greatly delighted with the sensation of being in air and superficially quite dry, and was particularly charmed with tea.

"And don't you have *tea?*" cried Miss Glendower, startled.

"How can we?"

"But do you really mean——?"

"I've never tasted tea before. How do you think we can boil a kettle?"

"What a strange—what a wonderful world it must be!" cried Adeline. And Mrs. Bunting said: "I can hardly *imagine* it without tea. It's worse than— I mean it reminds me—of abroad."

Mrs. Bunting was in the act of refilling the Sea Lady's cup. "I suppose," she said suddenly, "as you're not used to it— It won't affect your diges—" She glanced at Adeline and hesitated. "But it's China tea."

And she filled the cup.

"It's an inconceivable world to me," said Adeline. "Quite."

Her dark eyes rested thoughtfully on the Sea Lady for a space. "Inconceivable," she repeated, for, in that unaccountable way in which a whisper will attract attention that a turmoil fails to arouse, the tea had opened her eyes far more than the tail.

The Sea Lady looked at her with sudden frankness. "And think how wonderful all this must seem to *me!*" she remarked.

But Adeline's imagination was aroused for the moment and she was not to be put aside by the Sea Lady's terrestrial impressions. She pierced—for a moment or so—the ladylike serenity, the assumption of a terrestrial fashion of mind that was imposing so successfully upon Mrs. Bunting. "It must be," she said, "the strangest world." And she stopped invitingly. . . .

She could not go beyond that and the Sea Lady would not help her.

There was a pause, a silent eager search for topics. Apropos of the Niphetos roses on the table they talked of flowers and Miss Glendower ventured: "You have your anemones too! How beautiful they must be amidst the rocks!"

And the Sea Lady said they were very pretty—especially the cultivated sorts. . . .

"And the fishes," said Mrs. Bunting. "How wonderful it must be to see the fishes!"

"Some of them," volunteered the Sea Lady, "will come and feed out of one's hand."

Mrs. Bunting made a little coo of approval. She was reminded of chrysanthemum shows and the outside of the Royal Academy exhibition and she was one of those people to whom only the familiar is really satisfying. She had a momentary vision of the abyss as a sort of diverticulum of Piccadilly and the Temple, a place unexpectedly rational and comfortable. There was a kink for a time about a little matter of illumination, but it recurred to Mrs. Bunting only long after. The Sea Lady had turned from Miss Glendower's interrogative gravity of expression to the sunlight.

"The sunlight seems so golden here," said the Sea Lady. "Is it always golden?"

"You have that beautiful greenery-blue shimmer I suppose," said Miss Glendower, "that one catches sometimes ever so faintly in aquaria——"

"One lives deeper than that," said the Sea Lady. "Everything is phosphorescent, you know, a mile or so down, and it's like—I hardly know. As towns look at night—only brighter. Like piers and things like that."

"Really!" said Mrs. Bunting, with the Strand after the theaters in her head. "Quite bright?"

"Oh, quite," said the Sea Lady.

"But—" struggled Adeline, "is it never put out?"

"It's so different," said the Sea Lady.

"That's why it is so interesting," said Adeline.

"There are no nights and days, you know. No time nor anything of that sort."

"Now that's very queer," said Mrs. Bunting with Miss Glendower's teacup in her hand—they were both drinking quite a lot of tea absent-mindedly, in their interest in the Sea Lady. "But how do you tell when it's Sunday?"

"We don't—" began the Sea Lady. "At least not exactly—" And then—"Of course one hears the beautiful hymns that are sung on the passenger ships."

"Of course!" said Mrs. Bunting, having sung so in her youth and quite forgetting something elusive that she had previously seemed to catch.

But afterwards there came a glimpse of some more serious divergence—a glimpse merely. Miss Glendower hazarded a supposition that the sea people also had their Problems, and then it would seem the natural earnestness of her disposition overcame her proper attitude of ladylike superficiality and she began to ask questions. There can be no doubt that the Sea Lady was evasive, and Miss Glendower, perceiving that she had been a trifle urgent, tried to cover her error by expressing a general impression.

"I can't see it," she said, with a gesture that asked for sympathy. "One wants to see it, one wants to *be* it. One needs to be born a mer-child."

"A mer-child?" asked the Sea Lady.

"Yes— Don't you call your little ones——?"

"*What* little ones?" asked the Sea Lady.

She regarded them for a moment with a frank wonder, the undying wonder of the Immortals at that perpetual decay and death and replacement which is the gist of human life. Then at the expression of their faces she seemed to recollect. "Of course," she said, and then with a transition that made pursuit difficult, she agreed with Adeline. "It *is* different," she said. "It *is* wonderful. One feels so alike, you know, and so different. That's just where it *is* so wonderful. Do I look—? And yet you know I have never had my hair up, nor worn a dressing gown before to-day."

"What do you wear?" asked Miss Glendower. "Very charming things, I suppose."

"It's a different costume altogether," said the Sea Lady, brushing away a crumb.

Just for a moment Mrs. Bunting regarded her visitor fixedly. She had, I fancy, in that moment, an indistinct, imperfect glimpse of pagan possibilities. But there, you know, was the Sea Lady in her wrapper, so palpably a lady, with her pretty hair brought up to date and such a frank innocence in her eyes, that Mrs. Bunting's suspicions vanished as they came.

(But I am not so sure of Adeline.)

THE EPISODE OF THE VARIOUS JOURNALISTS

I

The remarkable thing is that the Buntings really carried out the program Mrs. Bunting laid down. For a time at least they positively succeeded in converting the Sea Lady into a credible human invalid, in spite of the galaxy of witnesses to the lady's landing and in spite of the severe internal dissensions that presently broke out. In spite, moreover, of the fact that one of the maids—they found out which only long after—told the whole story under vows to her very superior young man who told it next Sunday to a rising journalist who was sitting about on the Leas maturing a descriptive article. The rising journalist was incredulous. But he went about inquiring. In the end he thought it good enough to go upon. He found in several quarters a vague but sufficient rumor of a something; for the maid's young man was a conversationalist when he had anything to say.

Finally the rising journalist went and sounded the people on the two chief Folkestone papers and found the thing had just got to them. They were inclined to pretend they hadn't heard of it, after the fashion of local papers when confronted by the abnormal, but the atmosphere of enterprise that surrounded the rising journalist woke them up. He perceived he had done so and that he had no time to lose. So while they engaged in inventing representatives to inquire, he went off and telephoned to the *Daily Gunfire* and the *New Paper*. When they answered he was positive and earnest. He staked his reputation—the reputation of a rising journalist!

"I swear there's something up," he said. "Get in first—that's all."

He had some reputation, I say—and he had staked it. The *Daily Gunfire* was sceptical but precise, and the *New Paper* sprang a headline "A Mermaid at last!"

You might well have thought the thing was out after that, but it wasn't. There are things one doesn't believe even if they are printed in a halfpenny paper. To find the reporters hammering at their doors, so to speak, and fended off only for a time by a proposal that they should call again; to see their incredible secret glaringly in print, did indeed for a moment seem a hopeless exposure to both the Buntings and the Sea Lady. Already they could see the story spreading, could imagine the imminent rush of intimate inquiries, the tripod strides of a multitude of cameras, the crowds watching the windows, the horrors of a great publicity. All the Buntings and Mabel were aghast, simply aghast. Adeline was not so much aghast as excessively annoyed at this imminent and, so far as she was concerned, absolutely irrelevant publicity. "They will never dare—" she said, and "Consider how it affects Harry!" and at the earliest opportunity she retired to her own room. The others, with a certain disregard of her offense, sat around the Sea Lady's couch—she had scarcely touched her breakfast—and canvased the coming terror.

"They will put our photographs in the papers," said the elder Miss Bunting.

"Well, they won't put mine in," said her sister. "It's horrid. I shall go right off now and have it taken again."

"They'll interview the Ded!"

"No, no," said Mr. Bunting terrified. "Your mother——"

"It's your place, my dear," said Mrs. Bunting.

"But the Ded—" said Fred.

"I couldn't," said Mr. Bunting.

"Well, some one'll have to tell 'em anyhow," said Mrs. Bunting. "You know, they will——"

"But it isn't at all what I wanted," wailed the Sea Lady, with the *Daily Gunfire* in her hand. "Can't it be stopped?"

"You don't know our journalists," said Fred.

The tact of my cousin Melville saved the situation. He had dabbled in journalism and talked with literary fellows like myself. And literary fellows like myself are apt at times to be very free and outspoken about the press. He heard of the Buntings' shrinking terror of publicity as soon as he arrived, a perfect clamor—an almost exultant clamor indeed, of shrinking terror, and he caught the Sea Lady's eye and took his line there and then.

"It's not an occasion for sticking at trifles, Mrs. Bunting," he said. "But I think we can save the situation all the same. You're too hopeless. We must put our foot down at once; that's all. Let *me* see these reporter fellows and write to the London dailies. I think I can take a line that will settle them."

"Eh?" said Fred.

"I can take a line that will stop it, trust me."

"What, altogether?"

"Altogether."

"How?" said Fred and Mrs. Bunting. "You're not going to bribe them!"

"Bribe!" said Mr. Bunting. "We're not in France. You can't bribe a British paper."

(A sort of subdued cheer went around from the assembled Buntings.)

"You leave it to me," said Melville, in his element.

And with earnestly expressed but not very confident wishes for his success, they did.

He managed the thing admirably.

"What's this about a mermaid?" he demanded of the local journalists when they returned. They traveled together for company, being, so to speak, emergency journalists, compositors in their milder moments, and unaccustomed to these higher aspects of journalism. "What's this about a mermaid?" repeated my cousin, while they waived precedence dumbly one to another.

"I believe some one's been letting you in," said my cousin Melville. "Just imagine!—a mermaid!"

"That's what we thought," said the younger of the two emergency journalists. "We knew it was some sort of hoax, you know. Only the *New Paper* giving it a headline——"

"I'm amazed even Banghurst—" said my cousin Melville.

"It's in the *Daily Gunfire* as well," said the older of the two emergency journalists.

"What's one more or less of these ha'penny fever rags?" cried my cousin with a ringing scorn. "Surely you're not going to take your Folkestone news from mere London papers."

"But how did the story come about?" began the older emergency journalist.

"That's not my affair."

The younger emergency journalist had an inspiration. He produced a note book from his breast pocket. "Perhaps, sir, you wouldn't mind suggesting to us something we might say——"

My cousin Melville complied.

11

The rising young journalist who had first got wind of the business—who must not for a moment be confused with the two emergency journalists heretofore described—came to Banghurst next night in a state of strange exultation. "I've been through with it and I've seen her," he panted. "I waited about outside and saw her taken into the carriage. I've talked to one of the maids—I got into the house under pretense of being a telephone man to see their telephone—I spotted the wire—and it's a fact. A positive fact—she's a mermaid with a tail—a proper mermaid's tail. I've got here——"

He displayed sheets.

"Whaddyer talking about?" said Banghurst from his littered desk, eyeing the sheets with apprehensive animosity.

"The mermaid—there really *is* a mermaid. At Folkestone."

Banghurst turned away from him and pawed at his pen tray. "Whad if there is!" he said after a pause.

"But it's proved. That note you printed——"

"That note I printed was a mistake if there's anything of that sort going, young man." Banghurst remained an obstinate expansion of back.

"How?"

"We don't deal in mermaids here."

"But you're not going to let it drop?"

"I am."

"But there she is!"

"Let her be." He turned on the rising young journalist, and his massive face was unusually massive and his voice fine and full and fruity. "Do you think we're going to make our public believe anything simply because it's true? They know perfectly well what they are going to believe and what they aren't going to believe, and they aren't going to believe anything about mermaids—you bet your hat. I don't care if the whole damned beach was littered with mermaids—not the whole damned beach! We've got our reputation to keep up. See? . . . Look here!—you don't learn journalism as I hoped you'd do. It was you what brought in all that stuff about a discovery in chemistry——"

"It's true."

"Ugh!"

"I had it from a Fellow of the Royal Society——"

"I don't care if you had it from—anybody. Stuff that the public won't believe aren't facts. Being true only makes 'em worse. They buy our paper to swallow it and it's got to go down easy. When I printed you that note and headline I thought you was up to a lark. I thought you was on to a mixed bathing scandal or something of that sort—with juice in it. The sort of thing that *all* understand. You know when you went down to Folkestone you were going to describe what Salisbury and all the rest of them wear upon the Leas. And start a discussion on the acclimatization of the café. And all that. And then you get on to this (unprintable epithet) nonsense!"

"But Lord Salisbury—he doesn't go to Folkestone."

Banghurst shrugged his shoulders over a hopeless case. "What the deuce," he said, addressing his inkpot in plaintive tones, "does *that* matter?"

The young man reflected. He addressed Banghurst's back after a pause. His voice had flattened a little. "I might go over this and do it up as a lark perhaps. Make it a comic dialogue sketch with a man who really believed in it—or something like that. It's a beastly lot of copy to get slumped, you know."

"Nohow," said Banghurst. "Not in any shape. No! Why! They'd think it clever. They'd think you was making game of them. They hate things they think are clever!"

The young man made as if to reply, but Banghurst's back expressed quite clearly that the interview was at an end.

"Nohow," repeated Banghurst just when it seemed he had finished altogether.

"I may take it to the *Gunfire* then?"

Banghurst suggested an alternative.

"Very well," said the young man, heated, "the *Gunfire* it is."

But in that he was reckoning without the editor of the *Gunfire*.

III

It must have been quite soon after that, that I myself heard the first mention of the mermaid, little recking that at last it would fall to me to write her history. I was on one of my rare visits to London, and Micklethwaite was giving me lunch at the Penwiper Club, certainly one of the best dozen literary clubs in London. I noted the rising young journalist at a table near the door, lunching alone. All about him tables were vacant, though the other parts of the room were crowded. He sat with his face towards the door, and he kept looking up whenever any one came in, as if he expected some one who never came. Once distinctly I saw him beckon to a man, but the man did not respond.

"Look here, Micklethwaite," I said, "why is everybody avoiding that man over there? I noticed just now in the smoking-room that he seemed to be trying to get into conversation with some one and that a kind of taboo——"

Micklethwaite stared over his fork. "Ra-ther," he said.

"But what's he done?"

"He's a fool," said Micklethwaite with his mouth full, evidently annoyed. "Ugh," he said as soon as he was free to do so.

I waited a little while.

"What's he done?" I ventured.

Micklethwaite did not answer for a moment and crammed things into his mouth vindictively, bread and all sorts of things. Then leaning towards me in a confidential manner he made indignant noises which I could not clearly distinguish as words.

"Oh!" I said, when he had done.

"Yes," said Micklethwaite. He swallowed and then poured himself wine—splashing the tablecloth.

"He had *me* for an hour very nearly the other day."

"Yes?" I said.

"Silly fool," said Micklethwaite.

I was afraid it was all over, but luckily he gave me an opening again after gulping down his wine.

"He leads you on to argue," he said.

"That——?"

"That he can't prove it."

"Yes?"

"And then he shows you he can. Just showing off how damned ingenious he is."

I was a little confused. "Prove what?" I asked.

"Haven't I been telling you?" said Micklethwaite, growing very red. "About this confounded mermaid of his at Folkestone."

"He says there is one?"

"Yes, he does," said Micklethwaite, going purple and staring at me very hard. He seemed to ask mutely whether I of all people proposed to turn on him and back up this infamous scoundrel. I thought for a moment he would have apoplexy, but happily he remembered his duty as my host. So he turned very suddenly on a meditative waiter for not removing our plates.

"Had any golf lately?" I said to Micklethwaite, when the plates and the remains of the waiter had gone away. Golf always does Micklethwaite good except when he is actually playing. Then, I am told— If I were Mrs. Bunting I should break off and raise my eyebrows and both hands at this point, to indicate how golf acts on Micklethwaite when he is playing.

I turned my mind to feigning an interest in golf—a game that in truth I despise and hate as I despise and hate nothing else in this world. Imagine a great fat creature like Micklethwaite, a creature who ought to wear a turban and a long black robe to hide his grossness, whacking a little white ball for miles and miles with a perfect surgery of instruments, whacking it either with a babyish solemnity or a childish rage as luck may have decided, whacking away while his country goes to the devil, and incidentally training an innocent-eyed little boy to swear and be a tip-hunting loafer. That's golf! However, I controlled my all too facile sneer and talked of golf and the relative merits of golf links as I might talk to a child about buns or distract a puppy with the whisper of "rats," and when at last I could look at the rising young journalist again our lunch had come to an end.

I saw that he was talking with a greater air of freedom than it is usual to display to club waiters, to the man who held his coat. The man looked incredulous but respectful, and was answering shortly but politely.

When we went out this little conversation was still going on. The waiter was holding the rising young journalist's soft felt hat and the rising young journalist was fumbling in his coat pocket with a thick mass of papers.

"It's tremendous. I've got most of it here," he was saying as we went by. "I don't know if you'd care——"

"I get very little time for reading, sir," the waiter was replying.

THE QUALITY OF PARKER

I

So far I have been very full, I know, and verisimilitude has been my watchword rather than the true affidavit style. But if I have made it clear to the reader just how the Sea Lady landed and just how it was possible for her to land and become a member of human society without any considerable excitement on the part of that society, such poor pains as I have taken to tint and shadow and embellish the facts at my disposal will not have been taken in vain. She positively and quietly settled down with the Buntings. Within a fortnight she had really settled down so thoroughly that, save for her exceptional beauty and charm and the occasional faint touches of something a little indefinable in her smile, she had become a quite passable and credible human being. She was a cripple, indeed, and her lower limb was most pathetically swathed and put in a sort of case, but it was quite generally understood—I am afraid at Mrs. Bunting's initiative— that presently *they*—Mrs. Bunting said "they," which was certainly almost as far or even a little farther than legitimate prevarication may go—would be as well as ever.

"Of course," said Mrs. Bunting, "she will never be able to *bicycle* again——"

That was the sort of glamour she threw about it.

II

In Parker it is indisputable that the Sea Lady found—or at least had found for her by Mrs. Bunting—a treasure of the richest sort. Parker was still fallaciously young, but she had been maid to a lady from India who had been in a "case" and had experienced and overcome cross-examination. She had also been deceived by a young man, whom she had fancied greatly, only to find him walking out with another—contrary to her inflexible sense of correctness—in the presence of which all other things are altogether vain. Life she had resolved should have no further surprises for her. She looked out on its (largely improper) pageant with an expression of alert impartiality in her hazel eyes, calm, doing her specific duty, and entirely declining to participate further. She always kept her elbows down by her side and her hands always just in contact, and it was impossible for the most powerful imagination to conceive her under any circumstances as being anything but absolutely straight and clean and neat. And her voice was always under all circumstances low and wonderfully distinct—just to an infinitesimal degree indeed "mincing."

Mrs. Bunting had been a little nervous when it came to the point. It was Mrs. Bunting of course who engaged her, because the Sea Lady was so entirely without experience. But certainly Mrs. Bunting's nervousness was thrown away.

"You understand," said Mrs. Bunting, taking a plunge at it, "that—that she is an invalid."

"I *didn't*, Mem," replied Parker respectfully, and evidently quite willing to understand anything as part of her duty in this world.

"In fact," said Mrs. Bunting, rubbing the edge of the tablecloth daintily with her gloved finger and watching the operation with interest, "as a matter of fact, she has a mermaid's tail."

"Mermaid's tail! Indeed, Mem! And is it painful at all?"

"Oh, dear, no, it involves no inconvenience—nothing. Except—you understand, there is a need of—discretion."

"Of course, Mem," said Parker, as who should say, "there always is."

"We particularly don't want the servants——"

"The lower servants— No, Mem."

"You understand?" and Mrs. Bunting looked up again and regarded Parker calmly.

"Precisely, Mem!" said Parker, with a face unmoved, and so they came to the question of terms. "It all passed off *most* satisfactorily," said Mrs. Bunting, taking a deep breath at the mere memory of that moment. And it is clear that Parker was quite of her opinion.

She was not only discreet but really clever and handy. From the very outset she grasped the situation, unostentatiously but very firmly. It was Parker who contrived the sort of violin case for It, and who made the tea gown extension that covered the case's arid contours. It was Parker who suggested an invalid's chair for use indoors and in the garden, and a carrying chair for the staircase. Hitherto Fred Bunting had been on hand, at last even in excessive abundance, whenever the Sea Lady lay in need of masculine arms. But Parker made it clear at once that that was not at all in accordance with her ideas, and so earned the lifelong gratitude of Mabel Glendower. And Parker too spoke out for drives, and suggested with an air of rightness that left nothing else to be done, the hire of a carriage and pair for the season—to the equal delight of the Buntings and the Sea Lady. It was Parker who dictated the daily drive up to the eastern end of the Leas and the Sea Lady's transfer, and the manner of the Sea Lady's transfer, to the bath chair in which she promenaded the Leas. There seemed to be nowhere that it was pleasant and proper for the Sea Lady to go that Parker did not swiftly and correctly indicate it and the way to get to it, and there seems to have been nothing that it was really undesirable the Sea Lady should do and anywhere that it was really undesirable that she should go, that Parker did not at once invisibly but effectively interpose a bar. It was Parker who released the Sea Lady from being a sort of private and peculiar property in the Bunting household and carried her off to a becoming position in the world, when the crisis came. In little things as in great she failed not. It was she who made it luminous that the Sea Lady's card plate was not yet engraved and printed ("Miss Doris Thalassia Waters" was the pleasant and appropriate name with which the Sea Lady came primed), and who replaced the box of the presumably dank and drowned and dripping "Tom" by a jewel case, a dressing bag and the first of the Sea Lady's trunks.

On a thousand little occasions this Parker showed a sense of propriety that was penetratingly fine. For example, in the shop one day when "things" of an intimate sort were being purchased, she suddenly intervened.

"There are stockings, Mem," she said in a discreet undertone, behind, but not too vulgarly behind, a fluttering straight hand.

"*Stockings!*" cried Mrs. Bunting. "But——!"

"I think, Mem, she should have stockings," said Parker, quietly but very firmly.

And come to think of it, why *should* an unavoidable deficiency in a lady excuse one that can be avoided? It's there we touch the very quintessence and central principle of the proper life.

But Mrs. Bunting, you know, would never have seen it like that.

III

Let me add here, regretfully but with infinite respect, one other thing about Parker, and then she shall drop into her proper place.

I must confess, with a slight tinge of humiliation, that I pursued this young woman to her present situation at Highton Towers—maid she is to that eminent religious and social propagandist, the Lady Jane Glanville. There were certain details of which I stood in need, certain scenes and conversations of which my passion for verisimilitude had scarcely a crumb to go upon. And from first to last, what she must have seen and learned and inferred would amount practically to everything.

I put this to her frankly. She made no pretense of not understanding me nor of ignorance of certain hidden things. When I had finished she regarded me with a level regard.

"I couldn't think of it, sir," she said. "It wouldn't be at all according to my ideas."

"But!—It surely couldn't possibly hurt you now to tell me."

"I'm afraid I couldn't, sir."

"It couldn't hurt anyone."

"It isn't that, sir."

"I should see you didn't lose by it, you know."

She looked at me politely, having said what she intended to say.

And, in spite of what became at last very fine and handsome inducements, that remained the inflexible Parker's reply. Even after I had come to an end with my finesse and attempted to bribe her in the grossest manner, she displayed nothing but a becoming respect for my impregnable social superiority.

"I couldn't think of it, sir," she repeated. "It wouldn't be at all according to my ideas."

And if in the end you should find this story to any extent vague or incomplete, I trust you will remember how the inflexible severity of Parker's ideas stood in my way.

CHAPTER THE FIFTH
THE ABSENCE AND RETURN OF
MR. HARRY CHATTERIS

1

These digressions about Parker and the journalists have certainly led me astray from the story a little. You will, however, understand that while the rising young journalist was still in pursuit of information, Hope and Banghurst, and Parker merely a budding perfection, the carriage not even thought of, things were already developing in that bright little establishment beneath the evergreen oaks on the Folkestone Riviera. So soon as the minds of the Buntings ceased to be altogether focused upon this new and amazing social addition, they—of all people—had most indisputably discovered, it became at first faintly and then very clearly evident that their own simple pleasure in the possession of a guest so beautiful as Miss Waters, so solidly wealthy and—in a manner—so distinguished, was not entirely shared by the two young ladies who were to have been their principal guests for the season.

This little rift was perceptible the very first time Mrs. Bunting had an opportunity of talking over her new arrangements with Miss Glendower.

"And is she really going to stay with you all the summer?" said Adeline.

"Surely, dear, you don't mind?"

"It takes me a little by surprise."

"She's asked me, my dear——"

"I'm thinking of Harry. If the general election comes on in September—and every one seems to think it will— You promised you would let us inundate you with electioneering."

"But do you think she——"

"She will be dreadfully in the way."

She added after an interval, "She stops my working."

"But, my dear!"

"She's out of harmony," said Adeline.

Mrs. Bunting looked out of her window at the tamarisk and the sea. "I'm sure I wouldn't do anything to hurt Harry's prospects. You know how enthusiastic we all are. Randolph would do anything. But are you sure she will be in the way?"

"What else can she be?"

"She might help even."

"Oh, help!"

"She might canvas. She's very attractive, you know, dear."

"Not to me," said Miss Glendower. "I don't trust her."

"But to some people. And as Harry says, at election times every one who can do anything must be let do it. Cut them—do anything afterwards, but at the time—you know he talked of it when Mr. Fison and he were here. If you left electioneering only to the really nice people——"

"It was Mr. Fison said that, not Harry. And besides, she wouldn't help."

"I think you misjudge her there, dear. She has been asking——"

"To help?"

"Yes, and all about it," said Mrs. Bunting, with a transient pink. "She keeps asking questions about why we are having the election and what it is all about, and why Harry is a candidate and all that. She wants to go into it quite deeply. *I* can't answer half the things she asks."

"And that's why she keeps up those long conversations with Mr. Melville, I suppose, and why Fred goes about neglecting Mabel——"

"My dear!" said Mrs. Bunting.

"I wouldn't have her canvasing with us for anything," said Miss Glendower. "She'd spoil everything. She is frivolous and satirical. She looks at you with incredulous eyes, she seems to blight all one's earnestness. . . . I don't think you quite understand, dear Mrs. Bunting, what this election and my studies mean to me—and Harry. She comes across all that—like a contradiction."

"Surely, my dear! I've never heard her contradict."

"Oh, she doesn't contradict. But she— There is something about her— One feels that things that are most important and vital are nothing to her. Don't you feel it? She comes from another world to us."

Mrs. Bunting remained judicial. Adeline dropped to a lower key again. "I think," she said, "anyhow, that we're taking her very easily. How do we know what she is? Down there, out there, she may be anything. She may have had excellent reasons for coming to land——"

"My dear!" cried Mrs. Bunting. "Is that charity?"

"How do they live?"

"If she hadn't lived nicely I'm sure she couldn't behave so nicely."

"Besides—coming here! She had no invitation——"

"I've invited her now," said Mrs. Bunting gently.

"You could hardly help yourself. I only hope your kindness——"

"It's not a kindness," said Mrs. Bunting, "it's a duty. If she were only half as charming as she is. You seem to forget"—her voice dropped—"what it is she comes for."

"That's what I want to know."

"I'm sure in these days, with so much materialism about and such wickedness everywhere, when everybody who has a soul seems trying to lose it, to find any one who hadn't a soul and who is trying to find one——"

"But *is* she trying to get one?"

"Mr. Flange comes twice every week. He would come oftener, as you know, if there wasn't so much confirmation about."

"And when he comes he sits and touches her hand if he can, and he talks in his lowest voice, and she sits and smiles—she almost laughs outright at the things he says."

"Because he has to win his way with her. Surely Mr. Flange may do what he can to make religion attractive?"

"I don't believe she believes she will get a soul. I don't believe she wants one a bit."

She turned towards the door as if she had done.

Mrs. Bunting's pink was now permanent. She had brought up a son and two daughters, and besides she had brought down a husband to "My dear, how was *I* to know?" and when it was necessary to be firm—even with Adeline Glendower—she knew how to be firm just as well as anybody.

"My dear," she began in her very firmest quiet manner, "I am positive you misjudge Miss Waters. Trivial she may be—on the surface at any rate. Perhaps she laughs and makes fun a little. There are different ways of looking at things. But I am sure that at bottom she is just as serious, just as grave, as—any one. You judge her hastily. I am sure if you knew her better—as I do——"

Mrs. Bunting left an eloquent pause.

Miss Glendower had two little pink flushes in her cheeks. She turned with her hand on the door.

"At any rate," she said, "I am sure that Harry will agree with me that she can be no help to our cause. We have our work to do and it is something more than just vulgar electioneering. We have to develop and establish ideas. Harry has views that are new and wide-reaching. We want to put our whole strength into this work. Now especially. And her presence——"

She paused for a moment. "It is a digression. She divides things. She puts it all wrong. She has a way of concentrating attention about herself. She alters the values of things. She prevents my being single-minded, she will prevent Harry being single-minded——"

"I think, my dear, that you might trust my judgment a little," said Mrs. Bunting and paused.

Miss Glendower opened her mouth and shut it again, without speaking. It became evident finality was attained. Nothing remained to be said but the regrettable.

The door opened and closed smartly and Mrs. Bunting was alone.

Within an hour they all met at the luncheon table and Adeline's behaviour to the Sea Lady and to Mrs. Bunting was as pleasant and alert as any highly earnest and intellectual young lady's could be. And all that Mrs. Bunting said and did tended with what people call infinite tact—which really, you know, means a great deal more tact than is comfortable—to develop and expose the more serious aspect of the Sea Lady's mind. Mr. Bunting was unusually talkative and told them all about a glorious project he had just heard of, to cut out the rather shrubby and weedy front of the Leas and stick in something between a wine vault and the Crystal Palace as a Winter Garden— which seemed to him a very excellent idea indeed.

II

It is time now to give some impression of the imminent Chatteris, who for all his late appearance is really the chief human being in my cousin Melville's story. It happens that I met him with some frequency in my university days and afterwards ever and again I came upon him. He was rather a brilliant man at the university, smart without being vulgar and clever for all that. He was remarkably good-looking from the very onset of his manhood and without being in any way a showy spendthrift, was quite magnificently extravagant. There was trouble in his last year, something hushed up about a girl or woman in London, but his family had it all over with him, and his uncle, the Earl of Beechcroft, settled some of his bills. Not all—for the family is commendably free from sentimental excesses—but enough to make him comfortable again. The family is not a rich one and it further abounds in an extraordinary quantity of rather frowsy, loose-tongued aunts—I never knew a family quite so rich in old aunts. But Chatteris was so good-looking, easy-mannered, and clever, that they seemed to agree almost without discussion to pull him through. They hunted about for something that would be really remunerative without being laborious or too commercial; and meanwhile—after the extraordinary craving of his aunt, Lady Poynting Mallow, to see him acting had been overcome by the united efforts of the more religious section of his aunts—Chatteris set himself seriously to the higher journalism—that is to say, the journalism that dines anywhere, gets political tips after dinner, and is always acceptable—if only to avoid thirteen articles—in a half-crown review. In addition, he wrote some very passable verse and edited Jane Austen for the only publisher who had not already reprinted the works of that classic lady.

His verse, like himself, was shapely and handsome, and, like his face, it suggested to the penetrating eye certain reservations and indecisions. There was just that touch of refinement that is weakness in the public man. But as yet he was not a public man; he was known to be energetic and his work was gathering attention as always capable and occasionally brilliant. His aunts declared he was ripening, that any defect in vigor he displayed was the incompleteness of the process, and decided he should go to America, where vigor and vigorous opportunities abound, and there, I gather, he came upon something like a failure. Something happened, indeed, quite a lot happened. He came back unmarried—and *viâ* the South Seas, Australasia and India. And Lady Poynting Mallow publicly told him he was a fool, when he got back.

What happened in America, even if one does not consult contemporary American papers, is still very difficult to determine. There appear to have been the daughter of a millionaire and something like an engagement in the story. According to the *New York Yell*, one of the smartest, crispest, and altogether most representative papers in America, there was also the daughter of some one else, whom the *Yell* interviewed, or professed to interview, under the heading:

AN ARISTOCRATIC BRITISHER TRIFLES WITH
A PURE AMERICAN GIRL
INTERVIEW WITH THE VICTIM OF HIS HEARTLESS LEVITY

But this some one else was, I am inclined to think in spite of her excellently executed portrait, merely a brilliant stroke of modern journalism, the *Yell* having got wind of the sudden retreat of Chatteris and inventing a reason in preference to discovering one. Wensleydale tells me the true impetus to bolt was the merest trifle. The daughter of the millionaire, being a bright and spirited girl, had undergone interviewing on the subject of her approaching marriage, on marriage in general, on social questions of various sorts, and on the relations of the British and American peoples, and he seems to have found the thing in his morning paper. It took him suddenly and he lost his head. And once he started, he seems to have lacked the power of mind to turn about and come back. The affair was a mess, the family paid some more of his bills and shirked others, and Chatteris turned up in London again after a time, with somewhat diminished glory and a series of letters on Imperial Affairs, each headed with the quotation: "What do they know of England who only England know?"

Of course people of England learned nothing of the real circumstances of the case, but it was fairly obvious that he had gone to America and come back empty-handed.

And that was how, in the course of some years, he came to Adeline Glendower, of whose special gifts as his helper and inspiration you have already heard from Mrs. Bunting. When he became engaged to her, the family, which had long craved to forgive him—Lady Poynting Mallow as a matter of fact had done so—brightened wonderfully. And after considerable obscure activities he declared himself a philanthropic Liberal with open spaces in his platform, and in a position, and ready as a beginning, to try the quality of the conservative South.

He was away making certain decisive arrangements, in Paris and elsewhere, at the time of the landing of the Sea Lady. Before the matter was finally settled it was necessary that something should be said to a certain great public character, and then he was to return and tell Adeline. And every one was expecting him daily, including, it is now indisputable, the Sea Lady.

III

The meeting of Miss Glendower and her affianced lover on his return from Paris was one of those scenes in this story for which I have scarcely an inkling of the true details. He came to Folkestone and stopped at the Métropole, the Bunting house being full and the Métropole being the nearest hotel to Sandgate; and he walked down in the afternoon and asked for Adeline, which was pretty rather than correct. I gather that they met in the drawing-room, and as Chatteris closed the door behind him, I imagine there was something in the nature of a caress.

I must confess I envy the freedom of the novelist who can take you behind such a locked door as this and give you all that such persons say and do. But with the strongest will in the world to blend the little scraps of fact I have into a continuous sequence of events, I falter at this occasion. After all, I never saw Adeline at all until after all these things were over, and what is she now? A rather tall, a rather restless and active woman, very keen and obvious in public affairs—with something gone out of her. Melville once saw a gleam of that, but for the most part Melville never liked her; she had a wider grasp of things than he, and he was a little afraid of her; she was in some inexplicable way neither a pretty woman nor a "dear lady" nor a *grande dame* nor totally insignificant, and a heretic therefore in Melville's scheme of things. He gives me small material for that earlier Adeline. "She posed," he says; she was "political," and she was always reading Mrs. Humphry Ward.

The last Melville regarded as the most heinous offense. It is not the least of my cousin's weaknesses that he regards this great novelist as an extremely corrupting influence for intelligent girls. She makes them good and serious in the wrong way, he says. Adeline, he asserts, was absolutely built on her. She was always attempting to be the incarnation of *Marcella*. It was he who had perverted Mrs. Bunting's mind to adopt this fancy. But I don't believe for a moment in this idea of girls building themselves on heroines in fiction. These are matters of elective affinity, and unless some bullying critic or preacher sends us astray, we take each to our own novelist as the souls in the Swedenborgian system take to their hells. Adeline took to the imaginary *Marcella*. There was, Melville says, the strongest likeness in their mental atmosphere. They had the same defects, a bias for superiority—to use his expressive phrase—the same disposition towards arrogant benevolence, that same obtuseness to little shades of feeling that leads people to speak habitually of the "Lower Classes," and to think in the vein of that phrase. They certainly had the same virtues, a conscious and conscientious integrity, a hard nobility without one touch of magic, an industrious thoroughness. More than in anything else, Adeline delighted in her novelist's thoroughness, her freedom from impressionism, the patient resolution with which she went into the corners and swept under the mat of every incident. And it would be easy to argue from that, that Adeline behaved as Mrs. Ward's most characteristic heroine behaved, on an analogous occasion.

Marcella we know—at least after her heart was changed—would have clung to him. There would have been a moment of high emotion in which thoughts—of the highest class—mingled with the natural ambition of two people in the prime of life and power. Then she would have receded with a quick movement and listened with her beautiful hand pensive against her cheek, while Chatteris began to sum up the forces against him—to speculate on the action of this group and that. Something infinitely tender and maternal would have spoken in her, pledging her to the utmost help that love and a woman can give. She would have produced in Chatteris that exquisite mingled impression of grace, passion, self-yielding, which in all its infinite variations and repetitions made up for him the constant poem of her beauty.

But that is the dream and not the reality. So Adeline might have dreamt of behaving, but—she was not *Marcella*, and only wanting to be, and he was not only not Maxwell but he had no intention of being Maxwell anyhow. If he had had an opportunity of becoming

Maxwell he would probably have rejected it with extreme incivility. So they met like two unheroic human beings, with shy and clumsy movements and, I suppose, fairly honest eyes. Something there was in the nature of a caress, I believe, and then I incline to fancy she said "Well?" and I think he must have answered, "It's all right." After that, and rather allusively, with a backward jerk of the head at intervals as it were towards the great personage, Chatteris must have told her particulars. He must have told her that he was going to contest Hythe and that the little difficulty with the Glasgow commission agent who wanted to run the Radical ticket as a "Man of Kent" had been settled without injury to the party (such as it is). Assuredly they talked politics, because soon after, when they came into the garden side by side to where Mrs. Bunting and the Sea Lady sat watching the girls play croquet, Adeline was in full possession of all these facts. I fancy that for such a couple as they were, such intimation of success, such earnest topics, replaced, to a certain extent at any rate, the vain repetition of vulgar endearments.

The Sea Lady appears to have been the first to see them. "Here he is," she said abruptly.

"Whom?" said Mrs. Bunting, glancing up at eyes that were suddenly eager, and then following their glance towards Chatteris.

"Your other son," said the Sea Lady, jesting unheeded.

"It's Harry and Adeline!" cried Mrs. Bunting. "Don't they make a handsome couple?"

But the Sea Lady made no reply, and leaned back, scrutinising their advance. Certainly they made a handsome pair. Coming out of the veranda into the blaze of the sun and across the trim lawn towards the shadow of the ilex trees, they were lit, as it were, with a more glorious limelight, and displayed like actors on a stage more spacious than the stage of any theater. The figure of Chatteris must have come out tall and fair and broad, a little sunburnt, and I gather even then a little preoccupied, as indeed he always seemed to be in those latter days. And beside him Adeline, glancing now up at him and now towards the audience under the trees, dark and a little flushed, rather tall—though not so tall as *Marcella* seems to have been—and, you know, without any instructions from any novel-writer in the world, glad.

Chatteris did not discover that there was any one but Buntings under the tree until he was close at hand. Then the abrupt discovery of this stranger seems to have checked whatever he was prepared to say for his *début*, and Adeline took the center of the stage. Mrs. Bunting was standing up, and all the croquet players—except Mabel, who was winning—converged on Chatteris with cries of welcome. Mabel remained in the midst of what I understand is called a tea-party, loudly demanding that they should see her "play it out." No doubt if everything had gone well she would have given a most edifying exhibition of what croquet can sometimes be.

Adeline swam forward to Mrs. Bunting and cried with a note of triumph in her voice: "It is all settled. Everything is settled. He has won them all and he is to contest Hythe."

Quite involuntarily her eyes must have met the Sea Lady's.

It is of course quite impossible to say what she found there—or indeed what there was to find there then. For a moment they faced riddles, and then the Sea Lady turned her eyes with a long deferred scrutiny to the man's face, which she probably saw now closely for the first time. One wonders whether it is just possible that there may have been something, if it were no more than a gleam of surprise and inquiry, in that meeting of their eyes. Just for a moment she held his regard, and then it shifted inquiringly to Mrs. Bunting.

That lady intervened effusively with an "Oh! I forgot," and introduced them. I think they went through that without another meeting of the foils of their regard.

"You back?" said Fred to Chatteris, touching his arm, and Chatteris confirmed this happy guess.

The Bunting girls seemed to welcome Adeline's enviable situation rather than Chatteris as an individual. And Mabel's voice could be heard approaching. "Oughtn't they to see me play it out, Mr. Chatteris?"

"Hullo, Harry, my boy!" cried Mr. Bunting, who was cultivating a bluff manner. "How's Paris?"

"How's the fishing?" said Harry.

And so they came into a vague circle about this lively person who had "won them all"—except Parker, of course, who remained in her own proper place and was, I am certain, never to be won by anybody.

There was a handing and shifting of garden chairs.

No one seemed to take the slightest notice of Adeline's dramatic announcement. The Buntings were not good at thinking of things to say. She stood in the midst of the group like a leading lady when the other actors have forgotten their parts. Then every one woke up to this, as it were, and they went off in a volley. "So it's really all settled," said Mrs. Bunting; and Betty Bunting said, "There *is* to be an election then!" and Nettie said, "What fun!" Mr. Bunting remarked with a knowing air, "So you saw him then?" and Fred flung "Hooray!" into the tangle of sounds.

The Sea Lady of course said nothing.

"We'll give 'em a jolly good fight for it, anyhow," said Mr. Bunting.

"Well, I hope we shall do that," said Chatteris.

"We shall do more than that," said Adeline.

"Oh, yes!" said Betty Bunting, "we shall."

"I knew they would let him," said Adeline.

"If they had any sense," said Mr. Bunting.

Then came a pause, and Mr. Bunting was emboldened to lift up his voice and utter politics. "They are getting sense," he said. "They are learning that a party must have men, men of birth and training. Money and the mob—they've tried to keep things going by playing to fads and class jealousies. And the Irish. And they've had their lesson. How? Why,—we've stood aside. We've left 'em to faddists and fomenters—and the Irish. And here they are! It's a revolution in the party. We've let it down. Now we must pick it up again."

He made a gesture with his fat little hand, one of those fat pink little hands that appear to have neither flesh nor bones inside them but only sawdust or horse-hair. Mrs. Bunting leaned back in her chair and smiled at him indulgently.

"It is no common election," said Mr. Bunting. "It is a great issue."

The Sea Lady had been regarding him thoughtfully. "What is a great issue?" she asked. "I don't quite understand."

Mr. Bunting spread himself to explain to her. "This," he said to begin with. Adeline listened with a mingling of interest and impatience, attempting ever and again to suppress him and to involve Chatteris by a tactful interposition. But Chatteris appeared disinclined to be involved. He seemed indeed quite interested in Mr. Bunting's view of the case.

Presently the croquet quartette went back—at Mabel's suggestion—to their game, and the others continued their political talk. It became more personal at last, dealing soon quite specifically with all that Chatteris was doing and more particularly all that Chatteris was to do. Mrs. Bunting suddenly suppressed Mr. Bunting as he was offering advice, and Adeline took the burden of the talk again. She indicated vast purposes. "This election is merely the opening of a door," she said. When Chatteris made modest disavowals she smiled with a proud and happy consciousness of what she meant to make of him.

And Mrs. Bunting supplied footnotes to make it all clear to the Sea Lady. "He's so modest," she said at one point, and Chatteris pretended not to hear and went rather pink. Ever and again he attempted to deflect the talk towards the Sea Lady and away from himself, but he was hampered by his ignorance of her position.

And the Sea Lady said scarcely anything but watched Chatteris and Adeline, and more particularly Chatteris in relation to Adeline.

SYMPTOMATIC

1

M y cousin Melville is never very clear about his dates. Now this is greatly to be regretted, because it would be very illuminating indeed if one could tell just how many days elapsed before he came upon Chatteris in intimate conversation with the Sea Lady. He was going along the front of the Leas with some books from the Public Library that Miss Glendower had suddenly wished to consult, and which she, with that entire ignorance of his lack of admiration for her which was part of her want of charm for him, had bidden him bring her. It was in one of those sheltered paths just under the brow which give such a pleasant and characteristic charm to Folkestone, that he came upon a little group about the Sea Lady's bath chair. Chatteris was seated in one of the wooden seats that are embedded in the bank, and was leaning forward and looking into the Sea Lady's face; and she was speaking with a smile that struck Melville even at the time as being a little special in its quality—and she seems to have been capable of many charming smiles. Parker was a little distance away, where a sort of bastion projects and gives a wide view of the pier and harbor and the coast of France, regarding it all with a qualified disfavor, and the bath chairman was crumpled up against the bank lost in that wistful melancholy that the constant perambulation of broken humanity necessarily engenders.

My cousin slackened his pace a little and came up and joined them. The conversation hung at his approach. Chatteris sat back a little, but there seemed no resentment and he sought a topic for the three to discuss in the books Melville carried.

"Books?" he said.

"For Miss Glendower," said Melville.

"Oh!" said Chatteris.

"What are they about?" asked the Sea Lady.

"Land tenure," said Melville.

"That's hardly my subject," said the Sea Lady, and Chatteris joined in her smile as if he saw a jest.

There was a little pause.

"You are contesting Hythe?" said Melville.

"Fate points that way," said Chatteris.

"They threaten a dissolution for September."

"It will come in a month," said Chatteris, with the inimitable tone of one who knows.

"In that case we shall soon be busy."

"And *I* may canvas," said the Sea Lady. "I never have——"

"Miss Waters," explained Chatteris, "has been telling me she means to help us." He met Melville's eye frankly.

"It's rough work, Miss Waters," said Melville.

"I don't mind that. It's fun. And I want to help. I really do want to help—Mr. Chatteris."

"You know, that's encouraging."

"I could go around with you in my bath chair?"

"It would be a picnic," said Chatteris.

"I mean to help anyhow," said the Sea Lady.

"You know the case for the plaintiff?" asked Melville.

She looked at him.

"You've got your arguments?"

"I shall ask them to vote for Mr. Chatteris, and afterwards when I see them I shall remember them and smile and wave my hand. What else is there?"

"Nothing," said Chatteris, and shut the lid on Melville. "I wish I had an argument as good."

"What sort of people are they here?" asked Melville. "Isn't there a smuggling interest to conciliate?"

"I haven't asked that," said Chatteris. "Smuggling is over and past, you know. Forty years ago. It always has been forty years ago.

They trotted out the last of the smugglers,—interesting old man, full of reminiscences,—when there was a count of the Saxon Shore. He remembered smuggling—forty years ago. Really, I doubt if there ever was any smuggling. The existing coast guard is a sacrifice to a vain superstition."

"Why!" cried the Sea Lady. "Only about five weeks ago I saw quite near here——"

She stopped abruptly and caught Melville's eye. He grasped her difficulty.

"In a paper?" he suggested.

"Yes, in a paper," she said, seizing the rope he threw her.

"Well?" asked Chatteris.

"There is smuggling still," said the Sea Lady, with an air of some one who decides not to tell an anecdote that is suddenly found to be half forgotten.

"There's no doubt it happens," said Chatteris, missing it all. "But it doesn't appear in the electioneering. I certainly sha'n't agitate for a faster revenue cutter. However things may be in that respect, I take the line that they are very well as they are. That's my line, of course." And he looked out to sea. The eyes of Melville and the Sea Lady had an intimate moment.

"There, you know, is just a specimen of the sort of thing we do," said Chatteris. "Are you prepared to be as intricate as that?"

"Quite," said the Sea Lady.

My cousin was reminded of an anecdote.

The talk degenerated into anecdotes of canvasing, and ran shallow. My cousin was just gathering that Mrs. Bunting and Miss Bunting had been with the Sea Lady and had gone into the town to a shop, when they returned. Chatteris rose to greet them and explained—what had been by no means apparent before—that he was on his way to Adeline, and after a few further trivialities he and Melville went on together.

A brief silence fell between them.

"Who is that Miss Waters?" asked Chatteris.

"Friend of Mrs. Bunting," prevaricated Melville.

"So I gather. . . . She seems a very charming person."

"She is."

"She's interesting. Her illness seems to throw her up. It makes a passive thing of her, like a picture or something that's—imaginary. Imagined—anyhow. She sits there and smiles and responds. Her eyes—have something intimate. And yet——"

My cousin offered no assistance.

"Where did Mrs. Bunting find her?"

My cousin had to gather himself together for a second or so.

"There's something," he said deliberately, "that Mrs. Bunting doesn't seem disposed——"

"What can it be?"

"It's bound to be all right," said Melville rather weakly.

"It's strange, too. Mrs. Bunting is usually so disposed——"

Melville left that to itself.

"That's what one feels," said Chatteris.

"What?"

"Mystery."

My cousin shares with me a profound detestation of that high mystic method of treating women. He likes women to be finite—and nice. In fact, he likes everything to be finite—and nice. So he merely grunted.

But Chatteris was not to be stopped by that. He passed to a critical note. "No doubt it's all illusion. All women are impressionists, a patch, a light. You get an effect. And that is all you are meant to get, I suppose. She gets an effect. But how—that's the mystery. It's not merely beauty. There's plenty of beauty in the world. But not of these effects. The eyes, I fancy."

He dwelt on that for a moment.

"There's really nothing in eyes, you know, Chatteris," said my cousin Melville, borrowing an alien argument and a tone of analytical cynicism from me. "Have you ever looked at eyes through a hole in a sheet?"

"Oh, I don't know," said Chatteris. "I don't mean the mere physical eye. . . . Perhaps it's the look of health—and the bath chair. A bold discord. You don't know what's the matter, Melville?"

"How?"

"I gather from Bunting it's a disablement—not a deformity."

"He ought to know."

"I'm not so sure of that. You don't happen to know the nature of her disablement?"

"I can't tell at all," said Melville in a speculative tone. It struck him he was getting to prevaricate better.

The subject seemed exhausted. They spoke of a common friend whom the sight of the Métropole suggested. Then they did not talk at all for a time, until the stir and interest of the band stand was passed. Then Chatteris threw out a thought.

"Complex business—feminine motives," he remarked.

"How?"

"This canvasing. *She* can't be interested in philanthropic Liberalism. There's a difference in the type. And besides, it's a personal matter."

"Not necessarily, is it? Surely there's not such an intellectual gap between the sexes! If *you* can get interested——"

"Oh, I know."

"Besides, it's not a question of principles. It's the fun of electioneering."

"Fun!"

"There's no knowing what won't interest the feminine mind," said Melville, and added, "or what will."

Chatteris did not answer.

"It's the district visiting instinct, I suppose," said Melville. "They all have it. It's the canvasing. All women like to go into houses that don't belong to them."

"Very likely," said Chatteris shortly, and failing a reply from Melville, he gave way to secret meditations, it would seem still of a fairly agreeable sort.

The twelve o'clock gun thudded from Shornecliffe Camp.

"By Jove!" said Chatteris, and quickened his steps.

They found Adeline busy amidst her papers. As they entered she pointed reproachfully, yet with the protrusion of a certain *Marcella*-like undertone of sweetness, at the clock. The apologies of Chatteris were effusive and winning, and involved no mention of the Sea Lady on the Leas.

Melville delivered his books and left them already wading deeply into the details of the district organization that the local Liberal organizer had submitted.

II

A little while after the return of Chatteris, my cousin Melville and the Sea Lady were under the ilex at the end of the sea garden and—disregarding Parker (as every one was accustomed to do), who was in a garden chair doing some afternoon work at a proper distance—there was nobody with them at all. Fred and the girls were out cycling—Fred had gone with them at the Sea Lady's request—and Miss Glendower and Mrs. Bunting were at Hythe calling diplomatically on some rather horrid local people who might be serviceable to Harry in his electioneering.

Mr. Bunting was out fishing. He was not fond of fishing, but he was in many respects an exceptionally resolute little man, and he had taken to fishing every day in the afternoon after luncheon in order to break himself of what Mrs. Bunting called his "ridiculous habit" of getting sea-sick whenever he went out in a boat. He said that if fishing from a boat with pieces of mussels for bait after luncheon would not break the habit nothing would, and certainly it seemed at times as if it were going to break everything that was in him. But the habit escaped. This, however, is a digression.

These two, I say, were sitting in the ample shade under the evergreen oak, and Melville, I imagine, was in those fine faintly patterned flannels that in the year 1899 combined correctness with ease. He was no doubt looking at the shaded face of the Sea Lady, framed in a frame of sunlit yellow-green lawn and black-green ilex leaves—at least so my impulse for verisimilitude conceives it—and she at first was pensive and downcast that afternoon and afterwards she was interested and looked into his eyes. Either she must have suggested that he might smoke or else he asked. Anyhow, his cigarettes were produced. She looked at them with an arrested gesture, and he hung for a moment, doubtful, on her gesture.

"I suppose *you*—" he said.

"I never learned."

He glanced at Parker and then met the Sea Lady's regard.

"It's one of the things I came for," she said.

He took the only course.

She accepted a cigarette and examined it thoughtfully. "Down there," she said, "it's just one of the things— You will understand we get nothing but saturated tobacco. Some of the mermen— There's something they have picked up from the sailors. Quids, I think they call it. But that's too horrid for words!"

She dismissed the unpleasant topic by a movement, and lapsed into thought.

My cousin clicked his match-box.

She had a momentary doubt and glanced towards the house. "Mrs. Bunting?" she asked. Several times, I understand, she asked the same thing.

"She wouldn't mind—" said Melville, and stopped.

"She won't think it improper," he amplified, "if nobody else thinks it improper."

"There's nobody else," said the Sea Lady, glancing at Parker, and my cousin lit the match.

My cousin has an indirect habit of mind. With all general and all personal things his desperation to get at them obliquely amounts almost to a passion; he could no more go straight to a crisis than a cat could to a stranger. He came off at a tangent now as he was sitting forward and scrutinising her first very creditable efforts to draw. "I just wonder," he said, "exactly what it was you *did* come for."

She smiled at him over a little jet of smoke. "Why, this," she said.

"And hairdressing?"

"And dressing."

She smiled again after a momentary hesitation. "And all this sort of thing," she said, as if she felt she had answered him perhaps a little below his deserts. Her gesture indicated the house and the lawn and— my cousin Melville wondered just exactly how much else.

"Am I doing it right?" asked the Sea Lady.

"Beautifully," said my cousin with a faint sigh in his voice. "What do you think of it?"

"It was worth coming for," said the Sea Lady, smiling into his eyes.

"But did you really just come——?"

She filled in his gap. "To see what life was like on land here? . . . Isn't that enough?"

Melville's cigarette had failed to light. He regarded its blighted career pensively.

"Life," he said, "isn't all—this sort of thing."

"This sort of thing?"

"Sunlight. Cigarette smoking. Talk. Looking nice."

"But it's made up——"

"Not altogether."

"For example?"

"Oh, *you* know."

"What?"

"You know," said Melville, and would not look at her.

"I decline to know," she said after a little pause.

"Besides—" he said.

"Yes?"

"You told Mrs. Bunting—" It occurred to him that he was telling tales, but that scruple came too late.

"Well?"

"Something about a soul."

She made no immediate answer. He looked up and her eyes were smiling. "Mr. Melville," she said, innocently, "what *is* a soul?"

"Well," said my cousin readily, and then paused for a space. "A soul," said he, and knocked an imaginary ash from his extinct cigarette.

"A soul," he repeated, and glanced at Parker.

"A soul, you know," he said again, and looked at the Sea Lady with the air of a man who is handling a difficult matter with skilful care.

"Come to think of it," he said, "it's a rather complicated matter to explain——"

"To a being without one?"

"To any one," said my cousin Melville, suddenly admitting his difficulty.

He meditated upon her eyes for a moment.

"Besides," he said, "you know what a soul is perfectly well."

"No," she answered, "I don't."

"You know as well as I do."

"Ah! that may be different."

"You came to get a soul."

"Perhaps I don't want one. Why—if one hasn't one——?"

"Ah, *there!*" And my cousin shrugged his shoulders. "But really you know— It's just the generality of it that makes it hard to define."

"Everybody has a soul?"

"Every one."

"Except me?"

"I'm not certain of that."

"Mrs. Bunting?"

"Certainly."

"And Mr. Bunting?"

"Every one."

"Has Miss Glendower?"

"Lots."

The Sea Lady mused. She went off at a tangent abruptly.

"Mr. Melville," she said, "what is a union of souls?"

Melville flicked his extinct cigarette suddenly into an elbow shape and then threw it away. The phrase may have awakened some reminiscence. "It's an extra," he said. "It's a sort of flourish. . . . And sometimes it's like leaving cards by footmen—a substitute for the real presence."

There came a gap. He remained downcast, trying to find a way towards whatever it was that was in his mind to say. Conceivably, he did not clearly know what that might be until he came to it. The Sea Lady abandoned an attempt to understand him in favor of a more urgent topic.

"Do you think Miss Glendower and Mr. Chatteris——?"

Melville looked up at her. He noticed she had hung on the latter name. "Decidedly," he said. "It's just what they *would* do."

Then he spoke again. "Chatteris?" he said.

"Yes," said she.

"I thought so," said Melville.

The Sea Lady regarded him gravely. They scrutinized each other with an unprecedented intimacy. Melville was suddenly direct. It was a discovery that it seemed he ought to have made all along. He felt quite unaccountably bitter; he spoke with a twitch of the mouth and his voice had a note of accusation. "You want to talk about him."

She nodded—still grave.

"Well, *I* don't." He changed his note. "But I will if you wish it."

"I thought you would."

"Oh, *you* know," said Melville, discovering his extinct cigarette was within reach of a vindictive heel.

She said nothing.

"Well?" said Melville.

"I saw him first," she apologized, "some years ago."

"Where?"

"In the South Seas—near Tonga."

"And that is really what you came for?"

This time her manner was convincing. She admitted, "Yes."

Melville was carefully impartial. "He's sightly," he admitted, "and well-built and a decent chap—a decent chap. But I don't see why you——"

He went off at a tangent. "He didn't see you——?"

"Oh, no."

Melville's pose and tone suggested a mind of extreme liberality. "I don't see why you came," he said. "Nor what you mean to do. You see"—with an air of noting a trifling but valid obstacle—"there's Miss Glendower."

"Is there?" she said.

"Well, isn't there?"

"That's just it," she said.

"And besides after all, you know, why should you——?"

"I admit it's unreasonable," she said. "But why reason about it? It's a matter of the imagination——"

"For him?"

"How should I know how it takes him? That is what I *want* to know."

Melville looked her in the eyes again. "You know, you're not playing fair," he said.

"To her?"

"To any one."

"Why?"

"Because you are immortal—and unincumbered. Because you can do everything you want to do—and we cannot. I don't know why we cannot, but we cannot. Here we are, with our short lives and our little souls to save, or lose, fussing for our little concerns. And you, out of the elements, come and beckon——"

"The elements have their rights," she said. And then: "The elements are the elements, you know. That is what you forget."

"Imagination?"

"Certainly. That's *the* element. Those elements of your chemists——"

"Yes?"

"Are all imagination. There isn't any other." She went on: "And all the elements of your life, the life you imagine you are living, the little things you must do, the little cares, the extraordinary little duties, the day by day, the hypnotic limitations—all these things are a fancy that has taken hold of you too strongly for you to shake off. You daren't, you mustn't, you can't. To us who watch you——"

"You watch us?"

"Oh, yes. We watch you, and sometimes we envy you. Not only for the dry air and the sunlight, and the shadows of trees, and the feeling of morning, and the pleasantness of many such things, but because your lives begin and end—because you look towards an end."

She reverted to her former topic. "But you are so limited, so tied! The little time you have, you use so poorly. You begin and you end, and all the time between it is as if you were enchanted; you are afraid to do this that would be delightful to do, you must do that, though you know all the time it is stupid and disagreeable. Just think of the things—even the little things—you mustn't do. Up there on the Leas in this hot weather all the people are sitting in stuffy ugly clothes—ever so much too much clothes, hot tight boots, you know, when they have the most lovely pink feet, some of them—we *see*,—and they are all with little to talk about and nothing to look at, and bound not to do all sorts of natural things and bound to do all sorts of preposterous things. Why are they bound? Why are they letting life slip by them? Just as if they wouldn't all of them presently be dead! Suppose you were to go up there in a bathing dress and a white cotton hat——"

"It wouldn't be proper!" cried Melville.

"Why not?"

"It would be outrageous!"

"But any one may see you like that on the beach!"

"That's different."

"It isn't different. You dream it's different. And in just the same way you dream all the other things are proper or improper or good or bad to do. Because you are in a dream, a fantastic, unwholesome little dream. So small, so infinitely small! I saw you the other day dreadfully worried by a spot of ink on your sleeve—almost the whole afternoon."

My cousin looked distressed. She abandoned the ink-spot.

"Your life, I tell you, is a dream—a dream, and you can't wake out of it——"

"And if so, why do you tell me?"

She made no answer for a space.

"Why do you tell me?" he insisted.

He heard the rustle of her movement as she bent towards him.

She came warmly close to him. She spoke in gently confidential undertone, as one who imparts a secret that is not to be too lightly given. "Because," she said, "there are better dreams."

III

For a moment it seemed to Melville that he had been addressed by something quite other than the pleasant lady in the bath chair before him. "But how—?" he began and stopped. He remained silent with a perplexed face. She leaned back and glanced away from him, and when at last she turned and spoke again, specific realities closed in on him once more.

"Why shouldn't I," she asked, "if I want to?"

"Shouldn't what?"

"If I fancy Chatteris."

"One might think of obstacles," he reflected.

"He's not hers," she said.

"In a way, he's trying to be," said Melville.

"Trying to be! He has to be what he is. Nothing can make him hers. If you weren't dreaming you would see that." My cousin was silent. "She's not *real*," she went on. "She's a mass of fancies and vanities. She gets everything out of books. She gets herself out of a book. You can see her doing it here. . . . What is she seeking? What is she trying to do? All this work, all this political stuff of hers? She talks of the condition of the poor! What is the condition of the poor? A dreary tossing on the bed of existence, a perpetual fear of consequences that perpetually distresses them. Lives of anxiety they lead, because they do not know what a dream the whole thing is. Suppose they were not anxious and afraid. . . . And what does she care for the condition of the poor, after all? It is only a point of departure in her dream. In her heart she does not want their dreams to be happier, in her heart she has no passion for them, only her dream is that she should be prominently doing good, asserting herself, controlling their affairs amidst thanks and praise and blessings. *Her* dream! Of serious things!—a rout of phantoms pursuing a phantom ignis fatuus—the afterglow of a mirage. Vanity of vanities——"

"It's real enough to her."

"As real as she can make it, you know. But she isn't real herself. She begins badly."

"And he, you know——"

"He doesn't believe in it."

"I'm not so sure."

"I am—now."

"He's a complicated being."

"He will ravel out," said the Sea Lady.

"I think you misjudge him about that work of his, anyhow," said Melville. "He's a man rather divided against himself." He added abruptly, "We all are." He recovered himself from the generality. "It's vague, I admit, a sort of vague wish to do something decent, you know, that he has——"

"A sort of vague wish," she conceded; "but——"

"He means well," said Melville, clinging to his proposition.

"He means nothing. Only very dimly he suspects——"

"Yes?"

"What you too are beginning to suspect. . . . That other things may be conceivable even if they are not possible. That this life of yours is not everything. That it is not to be taken too seriously. Because . . . there are better dreams!"

The song of the sirens was in her voice; my cousin would not look at her face. "I know nothing of any other dreams," he said. "One has oneself and this life, and that is enough to manage. What other dreams can there be? Anyhow, we are in the dream—we have to accept it. Besides, you know, that's going off the question. We were talking of Chatteris, and why you have come for him. Why should you come, why should any one outside come—into this world?"

"Because we are permitted to come—we immortals. And why, if we choose to do so, and taste this life that passes and continues, as rain that falls to the ground, why should we not do it? Why should we abstain?"

"And Chatteris?"

"If he pleases me."

He roused himself to a Titanic effort against an oppression that was coming over him. He tried to get the thing down to a definite small case, an incident, an affair of considerations. "But look here, you know," he said. "What precisely do you mean to do if you get him? You don't seriously intend to keep up the game to that extent. You don't mean—positively, in our terrestrial fashion, you know—to marry him?"

The Sea Lady laughed at his recovery of the practical tone. "Well, why not?" she asked.

"And go about in a bath chair, and— No, that's not it. What *is* it?"

He looked up into her eyes, and it was like looking into deep water. Down in that deep there stirred impalpable things. She smiled at him.

"No!" she said, "I sha'n't marry him and go about in a bath chair. And grow old as all earthly women must. (It's the dust, I think, and the dryness of the air, and the way you begin and end.) You burn too fast, you flare and sink and die. This life of yours!—the illnesses and the growing old! When the skin wears shabby, and the light is out of the hair, and the teeth— Not even for love would I face it. No. . . . But then you know—" Her voice sank to a low whisper. "*There are better dreams.*"

"What dreams?" rebelled Melville. "What do you mean? What are you? What do you mean by coming into this life—you who pretend to be a woman—and whispering, whispering . . . to us who are in it, to us who have no escape."

"But there is an escape," said the Sea Lady.

"How?"

"For some there is an escape. When the whole life rushes to a moment—" And then she stopped. Now there is clearly no sense in this sentence to my mind, even from a lady of an essentially imaginary sort, who comes out of the sea. How can a whole life rush to a moment? But whatever it was she really did say, there is no doubt she left it half unsaid.

He glanced up at her abrupt pause, and she was looking at the house.

"Do . . . ris! Do . . . ris! Are you there?" It was Mrs. Bunting's voice floating athwart the lawn, the voice of the ascendant present, of invincibly sensible things. The world grew real again to Melville. He seemed to wake up, to start back from some delusive trance that crept upon him.

He looked at the Sea Lady as if he were already incredulous of the things they had said, as if he had been asleep and dreamed the talk. Some light seemed to go out, some fancy faded. His eye rested upon the inscription, "Flamps, Bath Chair Proprietor," just visible under her arm.

"We've got perhaps a little more serious than—" he said doubtfully, and then, "What you have been saying—did you exactly mean——?"

The rustle of Mrs. Bunting's advance became audible, and Parker moved and coughed.

He was quite sure they had been "more serious than——"

"Another time perhaps——"

Had all these things really been said, or was he under some fantastic hallucination?

He had a sudden thought. "Where's your cigarette?" he asked.

But her cigarette had ended long ago.

"And what have you been talking about so long?" sang Mrs. Bunting, with an almost motherly hand on the back of Melville's chair.

"Oh!" said Melville, at a loss for once, and suddenly rising from his chair to face her, and then to the Sea Lady with an artificially easy smile, "What *have* we been talking about?"

"All sorts of things, I dare say," said Mrs. Bunting, in what might almost be called an arch manner. And she honored Melville with a special smile—one of those smiles that are morally almost winks.

My cousin caught all the archness full in the face, and for four seconds he stared at Mrs. Bunting in amazement. He wanted breath. Then they all laughed together, and Mrs. Bunting sat down pleasantly and remarked, quite audibly to herself, "As if I couldn't guess."

IV

I gather that after this talk Melville fell into an extraordinary net of doubting. In the first place, and what was most distressing, he doubted whether this conversation could possibly have happened at all, and if it had whether his memory had not played him some trick in modifying and intensifying the import of it all. My cousin occasionally dreams conversations of so sober and probable a sort as to mingle quite perplexingly with his real experiences. Was this one of these occasions? He found himself taking up and scrutinising, as it were, first this remembered sentence and then that. Had she really said this thing and quite in this way? His memory of their conversation was never quite the same for two days together. Had she really and deliberately foreshadowed for Chatteris some obscure and mystical submergence?

What intensified and complicated his doubts most, was the Sea Lady's subsequent serene freedom from allusion to anything that might or might not have passed. She behaved just as she had always behaved; neither an added intimacy nor that distance that follows indiscreet confidences appeared in her manner.

And amidst this crop of questions arose presently quite a new set of doubts, as if he were not already sufficiently equipped. The Sea Lady alleged she had come to the world that lives on land, for Chatteris.

And then——?

He had not hitherto looked ahead to see precisely what would happen to Chatteris, to Miss Glendower, to the Buntings or any one when, as seemed highly probable, Chatteris was "got." There were other dreams, there was another existence, an elsewhere—and Chatteris was to go there! So she said! But it came into Melville's mind with a quite disproportionate force and vividness that once, long ago, he had seen a picture of a man and a mermaid, rushing downward through deep water. . . . Could it possibly be that sort of thing in the year eighteen hundred and ninety-nine? Conceivably, if she had said these things, did she mean them, and if she meant them, and this definite campaign of capture was in hand, what was an orderly, sane-living, well-dressed bachelor of the world to do?

Look on—until things ended in a catastrophe?

One figures his face almost aged. He appears to have hovered about the house on the Sandgate Riviera to a scandalous extent, failing always to get a sufficiently long and intimate tête-à-tête with the

Sea Lady to settle once for all his doubts as to what really had been said and what he had dreamed or fancied in their talk. Never had he been so exceedingly disturbed as he was by the twist this talk had taken. Never had his habitual pose of humorous acquiescence in life been quite so difficult to keep up. He became positively absent-minded. "You know if it's like that, it's serious," was the burden of his private mutterings. His condition was palpable even to Mrs. Bunting. But she misunderstood his nature. She said something. Finally, and quite abruptly, he set off to London in a state of frantic determination to get out of it all. The Sea Lady wished him good-bye in Mrs. Bunting's presence as if there had never been anything unusual between them.

I suppose one may contrive to understand something of his disturbance. He had made quite considerable sacrifices to the world. He had, at great pains, found his place and his way in it, he had imagined he had really "got the hang of it," as people say, and was having an interesting time. And then, you know, to encounter a voice, that subsequently insists upon haunting you with "*There are better dreams*"; to hear a tale that threatens complications, disasters, broken hearts, and not to have the faintest idea of the proper thing to do.

But I do not think he would have bolted from Sandgate until he had really got some more definite answer to the question, "*What* better dreams?" until he had surprised or forced some clearer illumination from the passive invalid, if Mrs. Bunting one morning had not very tactfully dropped a hint.

You know Mrs. Bunting, and you can imagine what she tactfully hinted. Just at that time, what with her own girls and the Glendower girls, her imagination was positively inflamed for matrimony; she was a matrimonial fanatic; she would have married anybody to anything just for the fun of doing it, and the idea of pairing off poor Melville to this mysterious immortal with a scaly tail seems to have appeared to her the most natural thing in the world.

Apropos of nothing whatever I fancy she remarked, "Your opportunity is now, Mr. Melville."

"My opportunity!" cried Melville, trying madly not to understand in the face of her pink resolution.

"You've a monopoly now," she cried. "But when we go back to London with her there will be ever so many people running after her."

I fancy Melville said something about carrying the thing too far. He doesn't remember what he did say. I don't think he even knew at the time.

However, he fled back to London in August, and was there so miserably at loose ends that he had not the will to get out of the place. On this passage in the story he does not dwell, and such verisimilitude as may be, must be supplied by my imagination. I imagine him in his charmingly appointed flat,—a flat that is light without being trivial, and artistic with no want of dignity or sincerity,—finding a loss of interest in his books, a loss of beauty in the silver he (not too vehemently) collects. I imagine him wandering into that dainty little bed-room of his and around into the dressing-room, and there, rapt in a blank contemplation of the seven-and-twenty pairs of trousers (all creasing neatly in their proper stretchers) that are necessary to his conception of a wise and happy man. For every occasion he has learned in a natural easy progress to knowledge, the exquisitely appropriate pair of trousers, the permissible upper garment, the becoming gesture and word. He was a man who had mastered his world. And then, you know, the whisper:—

"*There are better dreams.*"

"What dreams?" I imagine him asking, with a defensive note. Whatever transparence the world might have had, whatever suggestion of something beyond there, in the sea garden at Sandgate, I fancy that in Melville's apartments in London it was indisputably opaque.

And "Damn it!" he cried, "if these dreams are for Chatteris, why should she tell me? Suppose I had the chance of them— Whatever they are——"

He reflected, with a terrible sincerity in the nature of his will.

"No!" And then again, "No!

"And if one mustn't have 'em, why should one know about 'em and be worried by them? If she comes to do mischief, why shouldn't she do mischief without making me an accomplice?"

He walks up and down and stops at last and stares out of his window on the jaded summer traffic going Haymarket way.

He sees nothing of that traffic. He sees the little sea garden at Sandgate and that little group of people very small and bright and something—something hanging over them. "It isn't fair on them—or me—or anybody!"

Then you know, quite suddenly, I imagine him swearing.

I imagine him at his luncheon, a meal he usually treats with a becoming gravity. I imagine the waiter marking the kindly self-indulgence of his clean-shaven face, and advancing with that air of intimate participation the good waiter shows to such as he esteems. I figure the respectful pause, the respectful inquiry.

"Oh, anything!" cries Melville, and the waiter retires amazed.

V

To add to Melville's distress, as petty discomforts do add to all genuine trouble, his club-house was undergoing an operation, and was full of builders and decorators; they had gouged out its windows and gagged its hall with scaffolding, and he and his like were guests of a stranger club that had several members who blew. They seemed never to do anything but blow and sigh and rustle papers and go to sleep about the place; they were like blight-spots on the handsome plant of this host-club, and it counted for little with Melville, in the state he was in, that all the fidgety breathers were persons of eminent position. But it was this temporary dislocation of his world that brought him unexpectedly into a *quasi* confidential talk with Chatteris one afternoon, for Chatteris was one of the less eminent and amorphous members of this club that was sheltering Melville's club.

Melville had taken up *Punch*—he was in that mood when a man takes up anything—and was reading, he did not know exactly what. Presently he sighed, looked up, and discovered Chatteris entering the room.

He was surprised to see Chatteris, startled and just faintly alarmed, and Chatteris it was evident was surprised and disconcerted to see him. Chatteris stood in as awkward an attitude as he was capable of, staring unfavorably, and for a moment or so he gave no sign of recognition. Then he nodded and came forward reluctantly. His every movement suggested the will without the wit to escape. "You here?" he said.

"What are you doing away from Hythe at this time?" asked Melville.

"I came here to write a letter," said Chatteris.

He looked about him rather helplessly. Then he sat down beside Melville and demanded a cigarette. Suddenly he plunged into intimacy.

"It is doubtful whether I shall contest Hythe," he remarked.

"Yes?"

"Yes."

He lit his cigarette.

"Would you?" he asked.

"Not a bit of it," said Melville. "But then it's not my line."

"Is it mine?"

"Isn't it a little late in the day to drop it?" said Melville. "You've been put up for it now. Every one's at work. Miss Glendower——"

"I know," said Chatteris.

"Well?"

"I don't seem to want to go on."

"My dear man!"

"It's a bit of overwork perhaps. I'm off color. Things have gone flat. That's why I'm up here."

He did a very absurd thing. He threw away a quarter-smoked cigarette and almost immediately demanded another.

"You've been a little immoderate with your statistics," said Melville.

Chatteris said something that struck Melville as having somehow been said before. "Election, progress, good of humanity, public spirit. None of these things interest me really," he said. "At least, not just now."

Melville waited.

"One gets brought up in an atmosphere in which it's always being whispered that one should go for a career. You learn it at your mother's knee. They never give you time to find out what you really want, they keep on shoving you at that. They form your character. They rule your mind. They rush you into it."

"They didn't rush me," said Melville.

"They rushed me, anyhow. And here I am!"

"You don't want a career?"

"Well— Look what it is."

"Oh! if you look at what things are!"

"First of all, the messing about to get into the House. These confounded parties mean nothing—absolutely nothing. They aren't even decent factions. You blither to damned committees of damned tradesmen whose sole idea for this world is to get overpaid for their self-respect; you whisper and hobnob with local solicitors and get yourself seen about with them; you ask about the charities and institutions, and lunch and chatter and chum with every conceivable form of human conceit and pushfulness and trickery——"

He broke off. 'It isn't as if *they* were up to anything! They're working in their way, just as you are working in your way. It's the same game with all of them. They chase a phantom gratification, they toil and quarrel and envy, night and day, in the perpetual attempt to persuade themselves in spite of everything that they are real and a success——"

He stopped and smoked.

Melville was spiteful. "Yes," he admitted, "but I thought *your* little movement was to be something more than party politics and self-advancement——?"

He left his sentence interrogatively incomplete.

"The condition of the poor," he said.

"Well?" said Chatteris, regarding him with a sort of stony admission in his blue eyes.

Melville dodged the look. "At Sandgate," he said, "there was, you know, a certain atmosphere of belief——"

"I know," said Chatteris for the second time.

"That's the devil of it!" said Chatteris after a pause.

"If I don't believe in the game I'm playing, if I'm left high and dry on this shoal, with the tide of belief gone past me, it isn't *my* planning, anyhow. I know the decent thing I ought to do. I mean to do it; in the end I mean to do it; I'm talking in this way to relieve my mind. I've started the game and I must see it out; I've put my hand to the plough and I mustn't go back. That's why I came to London—to get it over with myself. It was running up against you, set me off. You caught me at the crisis."

"Ah!" said Melville.

"But for all that, the thing is as I said—none of these things interest me really. It won't alter the fact that I am committed to fight a phantom election about nothing in particular, for a party that's been dead ten years. And if the ghosts win, go into the Parliament as a constituent spectre. . . . There it is—as a mental phenomenon!"

He reiterated his cardinal article. "The interest is dead," he said, "the will has no soul."

He became more critical. He bent a little closer to Melville's ear. "It isn't really that I don't believe. When I say I don't believe in these things I go too far. I do. I know, the electioneering, the intriguing is a means to an end. There is work to be done, sound work, and important work. Only——"

Melville turned an eye on him over his cigarette end.

Chatteris met it, seemed for a moment to cling to it. He became absurdly confidential. He was evidently in the direst need of a confidential ear.

"I don't want to do it. When I sit down to it, square myself down in the chair, you know, and say, now for the rest of my life this is IT—this is your life, Chatteris; there comes a sort of terror, Melville."

"H'm," said Melville, and turned away. Then he turned on Chatteris with the air of a family physician, and tapped his shoulder three times as he spoke. "You've had too much statistics, Chatteris," he said.

He let that soak in. Then he turned about towards his interlocutor, and toyed with a club ash tray. "It's every day has overtaken you," he said. "You can't see the wood for the trees. You forget the spacious design you are engaged upon, in the heavy details of the moment. You are like a painter who has been working hard upon something very small and exacting in a corner. You want to step back and look at the whole thing."

"No," said Chatteris, "that isn't quite it."

Melville indicated that he knew better.

"I keep on, stepping back and looking at it," said Chatteris. "Just lately I've scarcely done anything else. I'll admit it's a spacious and noble thing—political work done well—only— I admire it, but it doesn't grip my imagination. That's where the trouble comes in."

"What *does* grip your imagination?" asked Melville. He was absolutely certain the Sea Lady had been talking this paralysis into Chatteris, and he wanted to see just how far she had gone. "For example," he tested, "are there—by any chance—other dreams?"

Chatteris gave no sign at the phrase. Melville dismissed his suspicion. "What do you mean—other dreams?" asked Chatteris.

"Is there conceivably another way—another sort of life—some other aspect——?"

"It's out of the question," said Chatteris. He added, rather remarkably, "Adeline's awfully good."

My cousin Melville acquiesced silently in Adeline's goodness.

"All this, you know, is a mood. My life is made for me—and it's a very good life. It's better than I deserve."

"Heaps," said Melville.

"Much," said Chatteris defiantly.

"Ever so much," endorsed Melville.

"Let's talk of other things," said Chatteris. "It's what even the street boys call *mawbid* nowadays to doubt for a moment the absolute final all-this-and-nothing-else-in-the-worldishness of whatever you happen to be doing."

My cousin Melville, however, could think of no other sufficiently interesting topic. "You left them all right at Sandgate?" he asked, after a pause.

"Except little Bunting."

"Seedy?"

"Been fishing."

"Of course. Breezes and the spring tides. . . . And Miss Waters?"

Chatteris shot a suspicious glance at him. He affected the offhand style. "*She's* quite well," he said. "Looks just as charming as ever."

"She really means that canvasing?"

"She's spoken of it again."

"She'll do a lot for you," said Melville, and left a fine wide pause.

Chatteris assumed the tone of a man who gossips.

"Who is this Miss Waters?" he asked.

"A very charming person," said Melville and said no more.

Chatteris waited and his pretense of airy gossip vanished. He became very much in earnest.

"Look here," he said. "Who is this Miss Waters?"

"How should *I* know?" prevaricated Melville.

"Well, you do know. And the others know. Who is she?"

Melville met his eyes. "Won't they tell you?" he asked.

"That's just it," said Chatteris.

"Why do you want to know?"

"Why shouldn't I know?"

"There's a sort of promise to keep it dark."

"Keep *what* dark?"

My cousin gestured.

"It can't be anything wrong?" My cousin made no sign.

"She may have had experiences?"

My cousin reflected a moment on the possibilities of the deep-sea life. "She has had them," he said.

"I don't care, if she has."

There came a pause.

"Look here, Melville," said Chatteris, "I want to know this. Unless it's a thing to be specially kept from me. . . . I don't like being among a lot of people who treat me as an outsider. What is this something about Miss Waters?"

"What does Miss Glendower say?"

"Vague things. She doesn't like her and she won't say why. And Mrs. Bunting goes about with discretion written all over her. And she herself looks at you— And that maid of hers looks— The thing's worrying me."

"Why don't you ask the lady herself?"

"How can I, till I know what it is? Confound it! I'm asking *you* plainly enough."

"Well," said Melville, and at the moment he had really decided to tell Chatteris. But he hung upon the manner of presentation. He thought in the moment to say, "The truth is, she is a mermaid." Then as instantly he perceived how incredible this would be. He always suspected Chatteris of a capacity for being continental and romantic. The man might fly out at him for saying such a thing of a lady.

A dreadful doubt fell upon Melville. As you know, he had never seen that tail with his own eyes. In these surroundings there came to him such an incredulity of the Sea Lady as he had not felt even when first Mrs. Bunting told him of her. All about him was an atmosphere of solid reality, such as one can breathe only in a first-class London club. Everywhere ponderous arm-chairs met the eye. There were massive tables in abundance and match-boxes of solid rock. The matches were of some specially large, heavy sort. On a ponderous elephant-legged green baize table near at hand were several copies of the *Times*, the current *Punch*, an inkpot of solid brass, and a paper weight of lead. *There are other dreams!* It seemed impossible. The breathing of an eminent person in a chair in the far corner became very distinct in that interval. It was heavy and resolute like the sound of a stone-mason's saw. It insisted upon itself as the touchstone of reality. It seemed to say that at the first whisper of a thing so utterly improbable as a mermaid it would snort and choke.

"You wouldn't believe me if I told you," said Melville.

"Well, tell me—anyhow."

My cousin looked at an empty chair beside him. It was evidently stuffed with the very best horse-hair that money could procure, stuffed with infinite skill and an almost religious care. It preached in the open invitation of its expanded arms that man does not live by bread alone—inasmuch as afterwards he needs a nap. An utterly dreamless chair!

Mermaids?

He felt that he was after all quite possibly the victim of a foolish delusion, hypnotized by Mrs. Bunting's beliefs. Was there not some more plausible interpretation, some phrase that would lie out bridgeways from the plausible to the truth?

"It's no good," he groaned at last.

Chatteris had been watching him furtively.

"Oh, I don't care a hang," he said, and shied his second cigarette into the massively decorated fireplace. "It's no affair of mine."

Then quite abruptly he sprang to his feet and gesticulated with an ineffectual hand.

"You needn't," he said, and seemed to intend to say many regrettable things. Meanwhile until his intention ripened he sawed the air with his ineffectual hand. I fancy he ended by failing to find a thing sufficiently regrettable to express the pungency of the moment. He flung about and went towards the door.

"Don't!" he said to the back of the newspaper of the breathing member.

"If you don't want to," he said to the respectful waiter at the door.

The hall-porter heard that he didn't care—he was damned if he did!

"He might be one of these here guests," said the hall-porter, greatly shocked. "That's what comes of lettin' 'em in so young."

VI

Melville overcame an impulse to follow him.

"Confound the fellow!" said he.

And then as the whole outburst came into focus, he said with still more emphasis, "Confound the fellow!"

He stood up and became aware that the member who had been asleep was now regarding him with malevolent eyes. He perceived it was a hard and invincible malevolence, and that no petty apologetics of demeanor could avail against it. He turned about and went towards the door.

The interview had done my cousin good. His misery and distress had lifted. He was presently bathed in a profound moral indignation, and that is the very antithesis of doubt and unhappiness. The more he thought it over, the more his indignation with Chatteris grew. That sudden unreasonable outbreak altered all the perspectives of the case. He wished very much that he could meet Chatteris again and discuss the whole matter from a new footing.

"Think of it!" He thought so vividly and so verbally that he was nearly talking to himself as he went along. It shaped itself into an outspoken discourse in his mind.

"Was there ever a more ungracious, ungrateful, unreasonable creature than this same Chatteris? He was the spoiled child of Fortune; things came to him, things were given to him, his very blunders brought more to him than other men's successes. Out of every thousand men, nine hundred and ninety-nine might well find food for envy in this way luck had served him. Many a one has toiled all his life and taken at last gratefully the merest fraction of all that had thrust itself upon this insatiable thankless young man. Even I," thought my cousin, "might envy him—in several ways. And then, at the mere first onset of duty, nay!—at the mere first whisper of restraint, this insubordination, this protest and flight!

"Think!" urged my cousin, "of the common lot of men. Think of the many who suffer from hunger——"

(It was a painful Socialistic sort of line to take, but in his mood of moral indignation my cousin pursued it relentlessly.)

"Think of many who suffer from hunger, who lead lives of unremitting toil, who go fearful, who go squalid, and withal strive, in a sort of dumb, resolute way, their utmost to do their duty, or at any rate what they think to be their duty. Think of the chaste poor women in the world! Think again of the many honest souls who aspire to the service of their kind, and are so hemmed about and preoccupied that they may not give it! And then this pitiful creature comes, with his mental gifts, his gifts of position and opportunity, the stimulus of great ideas, and a *fiancée*, who is not only rich and beautiful—she *is* beautiful!—but also the best of all possible helpers for him. And he turns away. It isn't good enough. It takes no hold upon his imagination, if you please. It isn't beautiful enough for him, and that's the plain truth of the matter. What does the man *want?* What does he expect? . . ."

My cousin's moral indignation took him the whole length of Piccadilly, and along by Rotten Row, and along the flowery garden walks almost into Kensington High Street, and so around by the Serpentine to his home, and it gave him such an appetite for dinner as he had not had for many days. Life was bright for him all that evening, and he sat down at last, at two o'clock in the morning, before a needlessly lit, delightfully fusillading fire in his flat to smoke one sound cigar before he went to bed.

"No," he said suddenly, "I am not *mawbid* either. I take the gifts the gods will give me. I try to make myself happy, and a few other people happy, too, to do a few little duties decently, and that is enough for me. I don't look too deeply into things, and I don't look too widely about things. A few old simple ideals——

"H'm.

"Chatteris is a dreamer, with an impossible, extravagant discontent. What does he dream of? . . . Three parts he is a dreamer and the fourth part—spoiled child."

"Dreamer . . ."

"Other dreams . . ."

"What other dreams could she mean?"

My cousin fell into profound musings. Then he started, looked about him, saw the time by his Rathbone clock, got up suddenly and went to bed.

THE CRISIS

I

The crisis came about a week from that time—I say about because of Melville's conscientious inexactness in these matters. And so far as the crisis goes, I seem to get Melville at his best. He was keenly interested, keenly observant, and his more than average memory took some excellent impressions. To my mind, at any rate, two at least of these people come out, fuller and more convincingly than anywhere else in this painfully disinterred story. He has given me here an Adeline I seem to believe in, and something much more like Chatteris than any of the broken fragments I have had to go upon, and amplify and fudge together so far. And for all such transient lucidities in this mysterious story, the reader no doubt will echo my Heaven be thanked!

Melville was called down to participate in the crisis at Sandgate by a telegram from Mrs. Bunting, and his first exponent of the situation was Fred Bunting.

"*Come down. Urgent. Please*," was the irresistible message from Mrs. Bunting. My cousin took the early train and arrived at Sandgate in the forenoon.

He was told that Mrs. Bunting was upstairs with Miss Glendower and that she implored him to wait until she could leave her charge. "Miss Glendower not well, then?" said Melville. "No, sir, not at all well," said the housemaid, evidently awaiting a further question. "Where are the others?" he asked casually. The three younger young ladies had gone to Hythe, said the housemaid, with a marked omission of the Sea Lady. Melville has an intense dislike of questioning servants on points at issue, so he asked nothing at all concerning Miss Waters. This general absence of people from the room of familiar occupation conveyed the same suggested warning of crisis as the telegram. The housemaid waited an instant longer and withdrew.

He stood for a moment in the drawing-room and then walked out upon the veranda. He perceived a richly caparisoned figure advancing towards him. It was Fred Bunting. He had been taking advantage of the general desertion of home to bathe from the house. He was wearing an umbrageous white cotton hat and a striped blanket, and a more aggressively manly pipe than any fully adult male would ever dream of smoking, hung from the corner of his mouth.

"Hello!" he said. "The mater sent for you?"

Melville admitted the truth of this theory.

"There's ructions," said Fred, and removed the pipe. The act offered conversation.

"Where's Miss Waters?"

"Gone."

"Back?"

"Lord, no! Catch her! She's gone to Lummidge's Hotel. With her maid. Took a suite."

"Why——"

"The mater made a row with her."

"Whatever for?"

"Harry."

My cousin stared at the situation.

"It broke out," said Fred.

"What broke out?"

"The row. Harry's gone daft on her, Addy says."

"On Miss Waters?"

"Rather. Mooney. Didn't care for his electioneering—didn't care for his ordinary nourishment. Loose ends. Didn't mention it to Adeline, but she began to see it. Asked questions. Next day, went off. London. She asked what was up. Three days' silence. Then—wrote to her."

Fred intensified all this by raising his eyebrows, pulling down the corners of his mouth and nodding portentously. "Eh?" he said, and then to make things clearer: "Wrote a letter."

"He didn't write to her about Miss Waters?"

"Don't know what he wrote about. Don't suppose he mentioned her name, but I dare say he made it clear enough. All I know is that everything in the house felt like elastic pulled tighter than it ought to be for two whole days—everybody in a sort of complicated twist—and then there was a snap. All that time Addy was writing letters to him and tearing 'em up, and no one could quite make it out. Everyone looked blue except the Sea Lady. She kept her own lovely pink. And at the end of that time the mater began asking things, Adeline chucked writing, gave the mater half a hint, mater took it all in in an instant and the thing burst."

"Miss Glendower didn't——?"

"No, the mater did. Put it pretty straight too—as the mater can. . . . *She* didn't deny it. Said she couldn't help herself, and that he was as much hers as Adeline's. I *heard* that," said Fred shamelessly. "Pretty thick, eh?—considering he's engaged. And the mater gave it her pretty straight. Said, 'I've been very much deceived in you, Miss Waters— very much indeed.' I heard her. . . ."

"And then?"

"Asked her to go. Said she'd requited us ill for taking her up when nobody but a fisherman would have looked at her."

"She said that?"

"Well, words to that effect."

"And Miss Waters went?"

"In a first-class cab, maid and boxes in another, all complete. Perfect lady. . . . Couldn't have believed if I hadn't seen it—the tail, I mean."

"And Miss Glendower?"

"Addy? Oh, she's been going it. Comes downstairs and does the pale-faced heroine and goes upstairs and does the broken-hearted part. *I* know. It's all very well. You never had sisters. You know——"

Fred held his pipe elaborately out of the way and protruded his face to a confidential nearness.

"I believe they half like it," said Fred, in a confidential half whisper. "Such a go, you know. Mabel pretty near as bad. And the girls. All making the very most they can of it. Me! I think Chatteris was the only man alive to hear 'em. *I* couldn't get up emotion as they do, if my feet were being flayed. Cheerful home, eh? For holidays."

"Where's—the principal gentleman?" asked Melville a little grimly. "In London?"

"Unprincipled gentleman, I call him," said Fred. "He's stopping down here at the Métropole. Stuck."

"Down here? Stuck?"

"Rather. Stuck and set about."

My cousin tried for sidelights. "What's his attitude?" he asked.

"Slump," said Fred with intensity.

"This little blow-off has rather astonished him," he explained. "When he wrote to say that the election didn't interest him for a bit, but he hoped to pull around——"

"You said you didn't know what he wrote."

"I do that much," said Fred. "He no more thought they'd have spotted that it meant Miss Waters than a baby. But women are so thundering sharp, you know. They're born spotters. How it'll all end——"

"But why has he come to the Métropole?"

"Middle of the stage, I suppose," said Fred.

"What's his attitude?"

"Says he's going to see Adeline and explain everything—and doesn't do it. . . . Puts it off. And Adeline, as far as I can gather, says that if he doesn't come down soon, she's hanged if she'll see him, much as her heart may be broken, and all that, if she doesn't. You know."

"Naturally," said Melville, rather inconsecutively. "And he doesn't?"

"Doesn't stir."

"Does he see—the other lady?"

"We don't know. We can't watch him. But if he does he's clever——"

"Why?"

"There's about a hundred blessed relatives of his in the place—came like crows for a corpse. I never saw such a lot. Talk about a man of good old family—it's decaying! I never saw such a high old family in my life. Aunts they are chiefly."

"Aunts?"

"Aunts. Say, they've rallied round him. How they got hold of it I don't know. Like vultures. Unless the mater— But they're here. They're all at him—using their influence with him, threatening to cut off legacies and all that. There's one old girl at Bate's, Lady Poynting Mallow—least bit horsey, but about as all right as any of 'em—who's been down here twice. Seems a trifle disappointed in Adeline. And there's two aunts at Wampach's—you know the sort that stop at Wampach's—regular hothouse flowers—a watering-potful of real icy cold water would kill both of 'em. And there's one come over from the Continent, short hair, short skirts—regular terror—she's at the Pavilion. They're all chasing round saying, 'Where is this woman-fish sort of thing? Let me peek!'"

"Does that constitute the hundred relatives?"

"Practically. The Wampachers are sending for a Bishop who used to be his schoolmaster——"

"No stone unturned, eh?"

"None."

"And has he found out yet——"

"That she's a mermaid? I don't believe he has. The pater went up to tell him. Of course, he was a bit out of breath and embarrassed. And Chatteris cut him down. 'At least let me hear nothing against her,' he said. And the pater took that and came away. Good old pater. Eh?"

"And the aunts?"

"They're taking it in. Mainly they grasp the fact that he's going to jilt Adeline, just as he jilted the American girl. The mermaid side they seem to boggle at. Old people like that don't take to a new idea all at once. The Wampach ones are shocked—but curious. They don't believe for a moment she really is a mermaid, but they want to know all about it. And the one down at the Pavilion simply said, 'Bosh! How can she breathe under water? Tell me that, Mrs. Bunting. She's some sort of person you have picked up, I don't know how, but mermaid she *cannot* be.' They'd be all tremendously down on the mater, I think, for picking her up, if it wasn't that they can't do without her help to bring Addy round again. Pretty mess all round, eh?"

"I suppose the aunts will tell him?"

"What?"

"About the tail."

"I suppose they will."

"And what then?"

"Heaven knows! Just as likely they won't."

My cousin meditated on the veranda tiles for a space.

"It amuses me," said Fred Bunting.

"Look here," said my cousin Melville, "what am I supposed to do? Why have I been asked to come?"

"I don't know. Stir it up a bit, I expect. Everybody do a bit—like the Christmas pudding."

"But—" said Melville.

"I've been bathing," said Fred. "Nobody asked me to take a hand and I didn't. It won't be a good pudding without me, but there you are! There's only one thing I can see to do——"

"It might be the right thing. What is it?"

"Punch Chatteris's head."

"I don't see how that would help matters."

"Oh, it wouldn't help matters," said Fred, adding with an air of conclusiveness, "There it is!" Then adjusting the folds of his blanket to a greater dignity, and replacing his long extinct large pipe between his teeth, he went on his way. The tail of his blanket followed him reluctantly through the door. His bare feet padded across the hall and became inaudible on the carpet of the stairs.

"Fred!" said Melville, going doorward with a sudden afterthought for fuller particulars.

But Fred had gone.

Instead, Mrs. Bunting appeared.

11

She appeared with traces of recent emotion. "I telegraphed," she said. "We are in dreadful trouble."

"Miss Waters, I gather——"

"She's gone."

She went towards the bell and stopped. "They'll get luncheon as usual," she said. "You will be wanting your luncheon."

She came towards him with rising hands. "You can *not* imagine," she said. "That poor child!"

"You must tell me," said Melville.

"I simply do not know what to do. I don't know where to turn." She came nearer to him. She protested. "All that I did, Mr. Melville, I did for the best. I saw there was trouble. I could see that I had been deceived, and I stood it as long as I could. I *had* to speak at last."

My cousin by leading questions and interrogative silences developed her story a little.

"And every one," she said, "blames me. Every one."

"Everybody blames everybody who does anything, in affairs of this sort," said Melville. "You mustn't mind that."

"I'll try not to," she said bravely. "*You* know, Mr. Melville——"

He laid his hand on her shoulder for a moment. "Yes," he said very impressively, and I think Mrs. Bunting felt better.

"We all look to you," she said. "I don't know what I should do without you."

"That's it," said Melville. "How do things stand? What am I to do?"

"Go to him," said Mrs. Bunting, "and put it all right."

"But suppose—" began Melville doubtfully.

"Go to her. Make her see what it would mean for him and all of us."

He tried to get more definite instructions. "Don't make difficulties," implored Mrs. Bunting. "Think of that poor girl upstairs. Think of us all."

"Exactly," said Melville, thinking of Chatteris and staring despondently out of the window.

"Bunting, I gather——"

"It is you or no one," said Mrs. Bunting, sailing over his unspoken words. "Fred is too young, and Randolph—! He's not diplomatic. He—he hectors."

"Does he?" exclaimed Melville.

"You should see him abroad. Often—many times I have had to interfere. . . . No, it is you. You know Harry so well. He trusts you. You can say things to him—no one else could say."

"That reminds me. Does *he* know——"

"We don't know. How can we know? We know he is infatuated, that is all. He is up there in Folkestone, and she is in Folkestone, and they may be meeting——"

My cousin sought counsel with himself.

"Say you will go?" said Mrs. Bunting, with a hand upon his arm.

"I'll go," said Melville, "but I don't see what I can do!"

And Mrs. Bunting clasped his hand in both of her own plump shapely hands and said she knew all along that he would, and that for coming down so promptly to her telegram she would be grateful to him so long as she had a breath to draw, and then she added, as if it were part of the same remark, that he must want his luncheon.

He accepted the luncheon proposition in an incidental manner and reverted to the question in hand.

"Do you know what his attitude——"

"He has written only to Addy."

"It isn't as if he had brought about this crisis?"

"It was Addy. He went away and something in his manner made her write and ask him the reason why. So soon as she had his letter saying he wanted to rest from politics for a little, that somehow he didn't seem to find the interest in life he thought it deserved, she divined everything——"

"Everything? Yes, but just what *is* everything?"

"That *she* had led him on."

"Miss Waters?"

"Yes."

My cousin reflected. So that was what they considered to be everything! "I wish I knew just where he stood," he said at last, and followed Mrs. Bunting luncheonward. In the course of that meal, which was *tête-à-tête*, it became almost unsatisfactorily evident what a great relief Melville's consent to interview Chatteris was to Mrs. Bunting. Indeed, she seemed to consider herself relieved from the greater portion of her responsibility in the matter, since Melville was bearing her burden. She sketched out her defense against the accusations that had no doubt been leveled at her, explicitly and implicitly.

"How was *I* to know?" she asked, and she told over again the story of that memorable landing, but with new, extenuating details. It was Adeline herself who had cried first, "She must be saved!" Mrs. Bunting made a special point of that. "And what else was there for me to do?" she asked.

And as she talked, the problem before my cousin assumed graver and yet graver proportions. He perceived more and more clearly the complexity of the situation with which he was entrusted. In the first place it was not at all clear that Miss Glendower was willing to receive back her lover except upon terms, and the Sea Lady, he was quite sure, did not mean to release him from any grip she had upon him. They were preparing to treat an elemental struggle as if it were an individual case. It grew more and more evident to him how entirely Mrs. Bunting overlooked the essentially abnormal nature of the Sea Lady, how absolutely she regarded the business as a mere every-day vacillation, a commonplace outbreak of that jilting spirit which dwells, covered deep, perhaps, but never entirely eradicated, in the heart of man; and how confidently she expected him, with a little tactful remonstrance and pressure, to restore the *status quo ante*.

As for Chatteris!—Melville shook his head at the cheese, and answered Mrs. Bunting abstractedly.

III

"She wants to speak to you," said Mrs. Bunting, and Melville with a certain trepidation went upstairs. He went up to the big landing with the seats, to save Adeline the trouble of coming down. She appeared dressed in a black and violet tea gown with much lace, and her dark hair was done with a simple carefulness that suited it. She was pale, and her eyes showed traces of tears, but she had a certain dignity that differed from her usual bearing in being quite unconscious.

She gave him a limp hand and spoke in an exhausted voice.

"You know—all?" she asked.

"All the outline, anyhow."

"Why has he done this to me?"

Melville looked profoundly sympathetic through a pause.

"I feel," she said, "that it isn't coarseness."

"Certainly not," said Melville.

"It is some mystery of the imagination that I cannot understand. I should have thought—his career at any rate—would have appealed . . ." She shook her head and regarded a pot of ferns fixedly for a space.

"He has written to you?" asked Melville.

"Three times," she said, looking up.

Melville hesitated to ask the extent of that correspondence, but she left no need for that.

"I had to ask him," she said. "He kept it all from me, and I had to force it from him before he would tell."

"Tell!" said Melville, "what?"

"What he felt for her and what he felt for me."

"But did he——?"

"He has made it clearer. But still even now. No, I don't understand."

She turned slowly and watched Melville's face as she spoke: "You know, Mr. Melville, that this has been an enormous shock to me. I suppose I never really knew him. I suppose I—idealized him. I thought he cared for—our work at any rate. . . . He *did* care for our work. He believed in it. Surely he believed in it."

"He does," said Melville.

"And then— But how can he?"

"He is—he is a man with rather a strong imagination."

"Or a weak will?"

"Relatively—yes."

"It is so strange," she sighed. "It is so inconsistent. It is like a child catching at a new toy. Do you know, Mr. Melville"—she hesitated—"all this has made me feel old. I feel very much older, very much wiser than he is. I cannot help it. I am afraid it is for all women . . . to feel that sometimes."

She reflected profoundly. "For *all* women— The child, man! I see now just what Sarah Grand meant by that."

She smiled a wan smile. "I feel just as if he had been a naughty child. And I—I worshipped him, Mr. Melville," she said, and her voice quivered.

My cousin coughed and turned about to stare hard out of the window. He was, he perceived, much more shockingly inadequate even than he had expected to be.

"If I thought she could make him happy!" she said presently, leaving a hiatus of generous self-sacrifice.

"The case is—complicated," said Melville.

Her voice went on, clear and a little high, resigned, impenetrably assured.

"But she would not. All his better side, all his serious side— She would miss it and ruin it all."

"Does he—" began Melville and repented of the temerity of his question.

"Yes?" she said.

"Does he—ask to be released?"

"No. . . . He wants to come back to me."

"And you——"

"He doesn't come."

"But do you—do you want him back?"

"How can I say, Mr. Melville? He does not say certainly even that he wants to come back."

My cousin Melville looked perplexed. He lived on the superficies of emotion, and these complexities in matters he had always assumed were simple, put him out.

"There are times," she said, "when it seems to me that my love for him is altogether dead. . . . Think of the disillusionment—the shock—the discovery of such weakness."

My cousin lifted his eyebrows and shook his head in agreement.

"His feet—to find his feet were of clay!"

There came a pause.

"It seems as if I have never loved him. And then—and then I think of all the things that still might be."

Her voice made him look up, and he saw that her mouth was set hard and tears were running down her cheeks.

It occurred to my cousin, he says, that he would touch her hand in a sympathetic manner, and then it occurred to him that he wouldn't. Her words rang in his thoughts for a space, and then he said somewhat tardily, "He may still be all those things."

"I suppose he may," she said slowly and without color. The weeping moment had passed.

"What is she?" she changed abruptly. "What is this being, who has come between him and all the realities of life? What is there about her—? And why should I have to compete with her, because he—because he doesn't know his own mind?"

"For a man," said Melville, "to know his own mind is—to have exhausted one of the chief interests in life. After that—! A cultivated extinct volcano—if ever it was a volcano."

He reflected egotistically for a space. Then with a secret start he came back to consider her.

"What is there," she said, with that deliberate attempt at clearness which was one of her antipathetic qualities for Melville—"what is there that she has, that she offers, that I——?"

Melville winced at this deliberate proposal of appalling comparisons. All the catlike quality in his soul came to his aid. He began to edge away, and walk obliquely and generally to shirk the issue. "My dear Miss Glendower," he said, and tried to make that seem an adequate reply.

"What *is* the difference?" she insisted.

"There are impalpable things," waived Melville. "They are above reason and beyond describing."

"But you," she urged, "you take an attitude, you must have an impression. Why don't you— Don't you see, Mr. Melville, this is very"—her voice caught for a moment—"very vital for me. It isn't kind of you, if you have impressions— I'm sorry, Mr. Melville, if I seem to be trying to get too much from you. I—I want to know."

It came into Melville's head for a moment that this girl had something in her, perhaps, that was just a little beyond his former judgments.

"I must admit, I have a sort of impression," he said.

"You are a man; you know him; you know all sorts of things—all sorts of ways of looking at things, I don't know. If you could go so far—as to be frank."

"Well," said Melville and stopped.

She hung over him as it were, as a tense silence.

"There *is* a difference," he admitted, and still went unhelped.

"How can I put it? I think in certain ways you contrast with her, in a way that makes things easier for her. He has—I know the thing sounds like cant, only you know, *he* doesn't plead it in defense—he has a temperament, to which she sometimes appeals more than you do."

"Yes, I know, but how?"

"Well——"

"Tell me."

"You are austere. You are restrained. Life—for a man like Chatteris—is schooling. He has something—something perhaps more worth having than most of us have—but I think at times—it makes life harder for him than it is for a lot of us. Life comes at him, with limitations and regulations. He knows his duty well enough. And you— You mustn't mind what I say too much, Miss Glendower—I may be wrong."

"Go on," she said, "go on."

"You are too much—the agent general of his duty."

"But surely!—what else——?"

"I talked to him in London and then I thought he was quite in the wrong. Since that I've thought all sorts of things—even that you might be in the wrong. In certain minor things."

"Don't mind my vanity now," she cried. "Tell me."

"You see you have defined things—very clearly. You have made it clear to him what you expect him to be, and what you expect him to do. It is like having built a house in which he is to live. For him, to go to her is like going out of a house, a very fine and dignified house, I admit, into something larger, something adventurous and incalculable. She is—she has an air of being—*natural*. She is as lax and lawless as the sunset, she is as free and familiar as the wind. She doesn't—if I may put it in this way—she doesn't love and respect him when he is this, and disapprove of him highly when he is that; she takes him altogether. She has the quality of the open sky, of the flight of birds, of deep tangled places, she has the quality of the high sea. That I think is what she is for him, she is the Great Outside. You—you have the quality——"

He hesitated.

"Go on," she insisted. "Let us get the meaning."

"Of an edifice. . . . I don't sympathize with him," said Melville. "I am a tame cat and I should scratch and mew at the door directly I got outside of things. I don't want to go out. The thought scares me. But he is different."

"Yes," she said, "he is different."

For a time it seemed that Melville's interpretation had hold of her. She stood thoughtful. Slowly other aspects of the thing came into his mind.

"Of course," she said, thinking as she looked at him. "Yes. Yes. That is the impression. That is the quality. But in reality— There are other things in the world beside effects and impressions. After all, that is—an analogy. It is pleasant to go out of houses and dwellings into the open air, but most of us, nearly all of us must live in houses."

"Decidedly," said Melville.

"He cannot— What can he do with her? How can he live with her? What life could they have in common?"

"It's a case of attraction," said Melville, "and not of plans."

"After all," she said, "he must come back—if I let him come back. He may spoil everything now; he may lose his election and be forced to start again, lower and less hopefully; he may tear his heart to pieces——"

She stopped at a sob.

"Miss Glendower," said Melville abruptly. "I don't think you quite understand."

"Understand what?"

"You think he cannot marry this—this being who has come among us?"

"How could he?"

"No—he couldn't. You think his imagination has wandered away from you—to something impossible. That generally, in an aimless way, he has cut himself up for nothing, and made an inordinate fool of himself, and that it's simply a business of putting everything back into place again."

He paused and she said nothing. But her face was attentive. "What you do not understand," he went on, "what no one seems to understand, is that she comes——"

"Out of the sea."

"Out of some other world. She comes, whispering that this life is a phantom life, unreal, flimsy, limited, casting upon everything a spell of disillusionment——"

"So that *he*——"

"Yes, and then she whispers, 'There are better dreams!'"

The girl regarded him in frank perplexity.

"She hints of these vague better dreams, she whispers of a way——"

"*What* way?"

"I do not know what way. But it is something—something that tears at the very fabric of this daily life."

"You mean——?"

"She is a mermaid, she is a thing of dreams and desires, a siren, a whisper and a seduction. She will lure him with her——"

He stopped.

"Where?" she whispered.

"Into the deeps."

"The deeps?"

They hung upon a long pause. Melville sought vagueness with infinite solicitude, and could not find it. He blurted out at last: "There can be but one way out of this dream we are all dreaming, you know."

"And that way?"

"That way—" began Melville and dared not say it.

"You mean," she said, with a pale face, half awakened to a new thought, "the way is——?"

Melville shirked the word. He met her eyes and nodded weakly.

"But how—?" she asked.

"At any rate"—he said hastily, seeking some palliative phrase—"at any rate, if she gets him, this little world of yours— There will be no coming back for him, you know."

"No coming back?" she said.

"No coming back," said Melville.

"But are you sure?" she doubted.

"Sure?"

"That it is so?"

"That desire is desire, and the deep the deep—yes."

"I never thought—" she began and stopped.

"Mr. Melville," she said, "you know I don't understand. I thought—I scarcely know what I thought. I thought he was trivial and foolish to let his thoughts go wandering. I agreed—I see your point—as to the difference in our effect upon him. But this—this suggestion that for him she may be something determining and final— After all, she——"

"She is nothing," he said. "She is the hand that takes hold of him, the shape that stands for things unseen."

"What things unseen?"

My cousin shrugged his shoulders. "Something we never find in life," he said. "Something we are always seeking."

"But what?" she asked.

Melville made no reply. She scrutinized his face for a time, and then looked out at the sunlight again.

"Do you want him back?" he said.

"I don't know."

"Do you want him back?"

"I feel as if I had never wanted him before."

"And now?"

"Yes. . . . But—if he will not come back?"

"He will not come back," said Melville, "for the work."

"I know."

"He will not come back for his self-respect—or any of those things."

"No."

"Those things, you know, are only fainter dreams. All the palace you have made for him is a dream. But——"

"Yes?"

"He might come back—" he said, and looked at her and stopped. He tells me he had some vague intention of startling her, rousing her, wounding her to some display of romantic force, some insurgence of passion, that might yet win Chatteris back, and then in that moment, and like a blow, it came to him how foolish such a fancy had been. There she stood impenetrably herself, limitedly intelligent, well-meaning, imitative, and powerless. Her pose, her face, suggested nothing but a clear and reasonable objection to all that had come to her, a critical antagonism, a steady opposition. And then, amazingly, she changed. She looked up, and suddenly held out both her hands, and there was something in her eyes that he had never seen before.

Melville took her hands mechanically, and for a second or so they stood looking with a sort of discovery into each other's eyes.

"Tell him," she said, with an astounding perfection of simplicity, "to come back to me. There can be no other thing than what I am. Tell him to come back to me!"

"And——?"

"Tell him *that*."

"Forgiveness?"

"No! Tell him I want him. If he will not come for that he will not come at all. If he will not come back for that"—she halted for a moment—"I do not want him. No! I do not want him. He is not mine and he may go."

His passive hold of her hands became a pressure. Then they dropped apart again.

"You are very good to help us," she said as he turned to go.

He looked at her. "You are very good to help me," she said, and then: "Tell him whatever you like if only he will come back to me! . . . No! Tell him what I have said." He saw she had something more to say, and stopped. "You know, Mr. Melville, all this is like a book newly opened to me. Are you sure——?"

"Sure?"

"Sure of what you say—sure of what she is to him—sure that if he goes on he will—" She stopped.

He nodded.

"It means—" she said and stopped again.

"No adventure, no incident, but a going out from all that this life has to offer."

"You mean," she insisted, "you mean——?"

"Death," said Melville starkly, and for a space both stood without a word.

She winced, and remained looking into his eyes. Then she spoke again.

"Mr. Melville, tell him to come back to me."

"And——?"

"Tell him to come back to me, or"—a sudden note of passion rang in her voice—"if I have no hold upon him, let him go his way."

"But—" said Melville.

"I know," she cried, with her face set, "I know. But if he is mine he will come to me, and if he is not— Let him dream his dream."

Her clenched hand tightened as she spoke. He saw in her face she would say no more, that she wanted urgently to leave it there. He turned again towards the staircase. He glanced at her and went down.

As he looked up from the bend of the stairs she was still standing in the light.

He was moved to proclaim himself in some manner her adherent, but he could think of nothing better than: "Whatever I can do I will." And so, after a curious pause, he departed, rather stumblingly, from her sight.

IV

After this interview it was right and proper that Melville should have gone at once to Chatteris, but the course of events in the world does occasionally display a lamentable disregard for what is right and proper. Points of view were destined to crowd upon him that day—for the most part entirely unsympathetic points of view. He found Mrs. Bunting in the company of a boldly trimmed bonnet in the hall, waiting, it became clear, to intercept him.

As he descended, in a state of extreme preoccupation, the boldly trimmed bonnet revealed beneath it a white-faced, resolute person in a duster and sensible boots. This stranger, Mrs. Bunting made apparent, was Lady Poynting Mallow, one of the more representative of the Chatteris aunts. Her ladyship made a few inquiries about Adeline with an eye that took Melville's measure, and then, after agreeing to a number of the suggestions Mrs. Bunting had to advance, proposed that he should escort her back to her hotel. He was much too exercised with Adeline to discuss the proposal. "I walk," she said. "And we go along the lower road."

He found himself walking.

She remarked, as the Bunting door closed behind them, that it was always a comfort to have to do with a man; and there was a silence for a space.

I don't think at that time Melville completely grasped the fact that he had a companion. But presently his meditations were disturbed by her voice. He started.

"I beg your pardon," he said.

"That Bunting woman is a fool," repeated Lady Poynting Mallow.

There was a slight interval for consideration.

"She's an old friend of mine," said Melville.

"Quite possibly," said Lady Poynting Mallow.

The position seemed a little awkward to Melville for a moment. He flicked a fragment of orange peel into the road. "I want to get to the bottom of all this," said Lady Poynting Mallow. "Who *is* this other woman?"

"What other woman?"

"*Tertium quid*," said Lady Poynting Mallow, with a luminous incorrectness.

"Mermaid, I gather," said Melville.

"What's the objection to her?"

"Tail."

"Fin and all?"

"Complete."

"You're sure of it?"

"Certain."

"How do you know?"

"I'm certain," repeated Melville with a quite unusual testiness.

The lady reflected.

"Well, there are worse things in the world than a fishy tail," she said at last.

Melville saw no necessity for a reply. "H'm," said Lady Poynting Mallow, apparently by way of comment on his silence, and for a space they went on.

"That Glendower girl is a fool too," she added after a pause.

My cousin opened his mouth and shut it again. How can one answer when ladies talk in this way? But if he did not answer, at any rate his preoccupation was gone. He was now acutely aware of the determined person at his side.

"She has means?" she asked abruptly.

"Miss Glendower?"

"No. I know all about her. The other?"

"The mermaid?"

"Yes, the mermaid. Why not?"

"Oh, *she*— Very considerable means. Galleons. Phœnician treasure ships, wrecked frigates, submarine reefs——"

"Well, that's all right. And now will you tell me, Mr. Melville, why shouldn't Harry have her? What if she is a mermaid? It's no worse than an American silver mine, and not nearly so raw and ill-bred."

"In the first place there's his engagement——"

"Oh, *that!*"

"And in the next there's the Sea Lady."

"But I thought she——"

"She's a mermaid."

"It's no objection. So far as I can see, she'd make an excellent wife for him. And, as a matter of fact, down here she'd be able to help him in just the right way. The member here—he'll be fighting—this Sassoon man—makes a lot of capital out of deep-sea cables. Couldn't be better. Harry could dish him easily. That's all right. Why shouldn't he have her?"

She stuck her hands deeply into the pockets of her dust-coat, and a china-blue eye regarded Melville from under the brim of the boldly trimmed bonnet.

"You understand clearly she is a properly constituted mermaid with a real physical tail?"

"Well?" said Lady Poynting Mallow.

"Apart from any question of Miss Glendower——"

"That's understood."

"I think that such a marriage would be impossible."

"Why?"

My cousin played round the question. "She's an immortal, for example, with a past."

"Simply makes her more interesting."

Melville tried to enter into her point of view. "You think," he said, "she would go to London for him, and marry at St. George's, Hanover Square, and pay for a mansion in Park Lane and visit just anywhere he liked?"

"That's precisely what she would do. Just now, with a Court that is waking up——"

"It's precisely what she won't do," said Melville.

"But any woman would do it who had the chance."

"She's a mermaid."

"She's a fool," said Lady Poynting Mallow.

"She doesn't even mean to marry him; it doesn't enter into her code."

"The hussy! What does she mean?"

My cousin made a gesture seaward. "That!" he said. "She's a mermaid."

"What?"

"Out there."

"Where?"

"There!"

Lady Poynting Mallow scanned the sea as if it were some curious new object. "It's an amphibious outlook for the family," she said after reflection. "But even then—if she doesn't care for society and it makes Harry happy—and perhaps after they are tired of—rusticating——"

"I don't think you fully realize that she is a mermaid," said Melville; "and Chatteris, you know, breathes air."

"That *is* a difficulty," admitted Lady Poynting Mallow, and studied the sunlit offing for a space.

"I don't see why it shouldn't be managed for all that," she considered after a pause.

"It can't be," said Melville with arid emphasis.

"She cares for him?"

"She's come to fetch him."

"If she wants him badly he might make terms. In these affairs it's always one or other has to do the buying. She'd have to *marry*—anyhow."

My cousin regarded her impenetrably satisfied face.

"He could have a yacht and a diving bell," she suggested; "if she wanted him to visit her people."

"They are pagan demigods, I believe, and live in some mythological way in the Mediterranean."

"Dear Harry's a pagan himself—so that doesn't matter, and as for being mythological—all good families are. He could even wear a diving dress if one could be found to suit him."

"I don't think that anything of the sort is possible for a moment."

"Simply because you've never been a woman in love," said Lady Poynting Mallow with an air of vast experience.

She continued the conversation. "If it's sea water she wants it would be quite easy to fit up a tank wherever they lived, and she could easily have a bath chair like a sitz bath on wheels. . . . Really, Mr. Milvain——"

"Melville."

"Mr. Melville, I don't see where your 'impossible' comes in."

"Have you seen the lady?"

"Do you think I've been in Folkestone two days doing nothing?"

"You don't mean you've called on her?"

"Dear, no! It's Harry's place to settle that. But I've seen her in her bath chair on the Leas, and I'm certain I've never seen any one who looked so worthy of dear Harry. *Never!*"

"Well, well," said Melville. "Apart from any other considerations, you know, there's Miss Glendower."

"I've never regarded her as a suitable wife for Harry."

"Possibly not. Still—she exists."

"So many people do," said Lady Poynting Mallow.

She evidently regarded that branch of the subject as dismissed. They pursued their way in silence.

"What I wanted to ask you, Mr. Milvain——"

"Melville."

"Mr. Melville, is just precisely where you come into this business?"

"I'm a friend of Miss Glendower."

"Who wants him back."

"Frankly—yes."

"Isn't she devoted to him?"

"I presume as she's engaged——"

"She ought to be devoted to him—yes. Well, why can't she see that she ought to release him for his own good?"

"She doesn't see it's for his good. Nor do I."

"Simply an old-fashioned prejudice because the woman's got a tail. Those old frumps at Wampach's are quite of your opinion."

Melville shrugged his shoulders.

"And so I suppose you're going to bully and threaten on account of Miss Glendower. . . . You'll do no good."

"May I ask what you are going to do?"

"What a good aunt always does."

"And that?"

"Let him do what he likes."

"Suppose he wants to drown himself?"

"My dear Mr. Milvain, Harry isn't a fool."

"I've told you she's a mermaid."

"Ten times."

A constrained silence fell between them.

It became apparent they were near the Folkestone Lift.

"You'll do no good," said Lady Poynting Mallow.

Melville's escort concluded at the lift station. There the lady turned upon him.

"I'm greatly obliged to you for coming, Mr. Milvain," she said; "and very glad to hear your views of this matter. It's a peculiar business, but I hope we're sensible people. You think over what I have said. As a friend of Harry's. You *are* a friend of Harry's?"

"We've known each other some years."

"I feel sure you will come round to my point of view sooner or later. It is so obviously the best thing for him."

"There's Miss Glendower."

"If Miss Glendower is a womanly woman, she will be ready to make any sacrifice for his good."

And with that they parted.

In the course of another minute Melville found himself on the side of the road opposite the lift station, regarding the ascending car. The boldly trimmed bonnet, vivid, erect, assertive, went gliding upward, a perfect embodiment of sound common sense. His mind was lapsing once again into disorder; he was stunned, as it were, by the vigor of her ladyship's view. Could any one not absolutely right be quite so clear and emphatic? And if so, what became of all that oppression of foreboding, that sinister promise of an escape, that whisper of "other dreams," that had dominated his mind only a short half-hour before?

He turned his face back to Sandgate, his mind a theater of warring doubts. Quite vividly he could see the Sea Lady as Lady Poynting Mallow saw her, as something pink and solid and smart and wealthy, and, indeed, quite abominably vulgar, and yet quite as vividly he recalled her as she had talked to him in the garden, her face full of shadows, her eyes of deep mystery, and the whisper that made all the world about him no more than a flimsy, thin curtain before vague and wonderful, and hitherto, quite unsuspected things.

V

Chatteris was leaning against the railings. He started violently at Melville's hand upon his shoulder. They made awkward greetings.

"The fact is," said Melville, "I—I have been asked to talk to you."

"Don't apologize," said Chatteris. "I'm glad to have it out with some one."

There was a brief silence.

They stood side by side—looking down upon the harbor. Behind, the evening band played remotely and the black little promenaders went to and fro under the tall electric lights. I think Chatteris decided to be very self-possessed at first—a man of the world.

"It's a gorgeous night," he said.

"Glorious," said Melville, playing up to the key set.

He clicked his cutter on a cigar. "There was something you wanted me to tell you——"

"I know all that," said Chatteris with the shoulder towards Melville becoming obtrusive. "I know everything."

"You have seen and talked to her?"

"Several times."

There was perhaps a minute's pause.

"What are you going to do?" asked Melville.

Chatteris made no answer and Melville did not repeat his question.

Presently Chatteris turned about. "Let's walk," he said, and they paced westward, side by side.

He made a little speech. "I'm sorry to give everybody all this trouble," he said with an air of having prepared his sentences; "I suppose there is no question that I have behaved like an ass. I am profoundly sorry. Largely it is my own fault. But you know—so far as the overt kick-up goes—there is a certain amount of blame attaches to our outspoken friend Mrs. Bunting."

"I'm afraid there is," Melville admitted.

"You know there are times when one is under the necessity of having moods. It doesn't help them to drag them into general discussion."

"The mischief's done."

"You know Adeline seems to have objected to the presence of—this sea lady at a very early stage. Mrs. Bunting overruled her. Afterwards when there was trouble she seems to have tried to make up for it."

"I didn't know Miss Glendower had objected."

"She did. She seems to have seen—ahead."

Chatteris reflected. "Of course all that doesn't excuse me in the least. But it's a sort of excuse for *your* being dragged into this bother."

He said something less distinctly about a "stupid bother" and "private affairs."

They found themselves drawing near the band and already on the outskirts of its territory of votaries. Its cheerful rhythms became insistent. The canopy of the stand was a focus of bright light, music-stands and instruments sent out beams of reflected brilliance, and a luminous red conductor in the midst of the lantern guided the ratatoo-tat, ratatoo-tat of a popular air. Voices, detached fragments of conversation, came to our talkers and mingled impertinently with their thoughts.

"I wouldn't 'ave no truck with 'im, not after that," said a young person to her friend.

"Let's get out of this," said Chatteris abruptly.

They turned aside from the high path of the Leas to the head of some steps that led down the declivity. In a few moments it was as if those imposing fronts of stucco, those many-windowed hotels, the electric lights on the tall masts, the band-stand and miscellaneous holiday British public, had never existed. It is one of Folkestone's best effects, that black quietness under the very feet of a crowd. They no longer heard the band even, only a remote suggestion of music filtered to them over the brow. The black-treed slopes fell from them to the surf below, and out at sea were the lights of many ships. Away to the westward like a swarm of fire-flies hung the lights of Hythe. The two men sat down on a vacant seat in the dimness. For a time neither spoke. Chatteris impressed Melville with an air of being on the defensive. He murmured in a meditative undertone, "I wouldn't 'ave no truck with 'im not after that."

"I will admit by every standard," he said aloud, "that I have been flappy and feeble and wrong. Very. In these things there is a prescribed and definite course. To hesitate, to have two points of view, is condemned by all right-thinking people. . . . Still—one has the two points of view. . . . You have come up from Sandgate?"

"Yes."

"Did you see Miss Glendower?"

"Yes."

"Talked to her? . . . I suppose— What do you think of her?"

His cigar glowed into an expectant brightness while Melville hesitated at his answer, and showed his eyes thoughtful upon Melville's face.

"I've never thought her—" Melville sought more diplomatic phrasing. "I've never found her exceptionally attractive before. Handsome, you know, but not—winning. But this time, she seemed . . . rather splendid."

"She is," said Chatteris, "she is."

He sat forward and began flicking imaginary ash from the end of his cigar.

"She *is* splendid," he admitted. "You—only begin to imagine. You don't, my dear man, know that girl. She is not—quite—in your line. She is, I assure you, the straightest and cleanest and clearest human being I have ever met. She believes so firmly, she does right so simply, there is a sort of queenly benevolence, a sort of integrity of benevolence——"

He left the sentence unfinished, as if unfinished it completely expressed his thought.

"She wants you to go back to her," said Melville bluntly.

"I know," said Chatteris and flicked again at that ghostly ash. "She has written that. . . . That's just where her complete magnificence comes in. She doesn't fence and fool about, as the she-women do. She doesn't squawk and say, 'You've insulted me and everything's at an end;' and she doesn't squawk and say, 'For God's sake come back to me!' *She* doesn't say, she 'won't 'ave no truck with me not after this.' She writes—straight. I don't believe, Melville, I half knew her until all this business came up. She comes out. . . . Before that it was, as you said, and I quite perceive—I perceived all along—a little too—statistical."

He became meditative, and his cigar glow waned and presently vanished altogether.

"You are going back?"

"By Jove! *Yes.*"

Melville stirred slightly and then they both sat rigidly quiet for a space. Then abruptly Chatteris flung away his extinct cigar. He seemed to fling many other things away with that dim gesture. "Of course," he said, "I shall go back.

"It is not my fault," he insisted, "that this trouble, this separation, has ever arisen. I was moody, I was preoccupied, I know—things had got into my head. But if I'd been left alone. . . .

"I have been forced into this position," he summarized.

"You understand," said Melville, "that—though I think matters are indefined and distressing just now—I don't attach blame—anywhere."

"You're open-minded," said Chatteris. "That's just your way. And I can imagine how all this upset and discomfort distresses you. You're awfully good to keep so open-minded and not to consider me an utter outcast, an ill-regulated disturber of the order of the world."

"It's a distressing state of affairs," said Melville. "But perhaps I understand the forces pulling at you—better than you imagine."

"They're very simple, I suppose."

"Very."

"And yet——?"

"Well?"

He seemed to hesitate at a dangerous topic. "The other," he said. Melville's silence bade him go on.

He plunged from his prepared attitude. "What is it? Why should—this being—come into my life, as she has done, if it *is* so simple? What is there about her, or me, that has pulled me so astray? She has, you know. Here we are at sixes and sevens! It's not the situation, it's the mental conflict. Why am I pulled about? She has got into my imagination. How? I haven't the remotest idea."

"She's beautiful," meditated Melville.

"She's beautiful certainly. But so is Miss Glendower."

"She's very beautiful. I'm not blind, Chatteris. She's beautiful in a different way."

"Yes, but that's only the name for the effect. *Why* is she very beautiful?"

Melville shrugged his shoulders.

"She's not beautiful to every one."

"You mean?"

"Bunting keeps calm."

"Oh—*he*——!"

"And other people don't seem to see it—as I do."

"Some people seem to see no beauty at all, as we do. With emotion, that is."

"Why do we?"

"We see—finer."

"Do we? Is it finer? Why should it be finer to see beauty where it is fatal to us to see it? Why? Unless we are to believe there is no reason in things, why should this—impossibility, be beautiful to any one anyhow? Put it as a matter of reason, Melville. Why should *her* smile be so sweet to me, why should *her* voice move me! Why her's and not Adeline's? Adeline has straight eyes and clear eyes and fine eyes, and all the difference there can be, what is it? An infinitesimal curving of the lid, an infinitesimal difference in the lashes—and it shatters everything—in this way. Who could measure the difference, who could tell the quality that makes me *swim* in the sound of her voice. . . . The difference? After all, it's a visible thing, it's a material thing! It's in my eyes. By Jove!" he laughed abruptly. "Imagine old Helmholtz trying to gauge it with a battery of resonators, or Spencer in the light of Evolution and the Environment explaining it away!"

"These things are beyond measurement," said Melville.

"Not if you measure them by their effect," said Chatteris. "And anyhow, why do they take us? That is the question I can't get away from just now."

My cousin meditated, no doubt with his hands deep in his trousers' pockets. "It is illusion," he said. "It is a sort of glamour. After all, look at it squarely. What is she? What can she give you? She promises you vague somethings. . . . She is a snare, she is deception. She is the beautiful mask of death."

"Yes," said Chatteris. "I know."

And then again, "I know.

"There is nothing for me to learn about that," he said. "But why— why should the mask of death be beautiful? After all— We get our duty by good hard reasoning. Why should reason and justice carry everything? Perhaps after all there are things beyond our reason, perhaps after all desire has a claim on us?"

He stopped interrogatively and Melville was profound. "I think," said my cousin at last, "Desire *has* a claim on us. Beauty, at any rate——

"I mean," he explained, "we are human beings. We are matter with minds growing out of ourselves. We reach downward into the beautiful wonderland of matter, and upward to something—" He stopped, from sheer dissatisfaction with the image. "In another direction, anyhow," he tried feebly. He jumped at something that was not quite his meaning. "Man is a sort of half-way house—he must compromise."

"As you do?"

"Well. Yes. I try to strike a balance."

"A few old engravings—good, I suppose—a little luxury in furniture and flowers, a few things that come within your means. Art—in moderation, and a few kindly acts of the pleasanter sort, a certain respect for truth; duty—also in moderation. Eh? It's just that even balance that I cannot contrive. I cannot sit down to the oatmeal of this daily life and wash it down with a temperate draught of beauty and water. Art! . . . I suppose I'm voracious, I'm one of the unfit—for the civilized stage. I've sat down once, I've sat down twice, to perfectly sane, secure, and reasonable things. . . . It's not my way."

He repeated, "It's not my way."

Melville, I think, said nothing to that. He was distracted from the immediate topic by the discussion of his own way of living. He was lost in egotistical comparisons. No doubt he was on the verge of saying, as most of us would have been under the circumstances: "I don't think you quite understand my position."

"But, after all, what is the good of talking in this way?" exclaimed Chatteris abruptly. "I am simply trying to elevate the whole business by dragging in these wider questions. It's justification, when I didn't mean to justify. I have to choose between life with Adeline and this woman out of the sea."

"Who is Death."

"How do I know she is Death?"

"But you said you had made your choice!"

"I have."

He seemed to recollect.

"I have," he corroborated. "I told you. I am going back to see Miss Glendower to-morrow.

"Yes." He recalled further portions of what I believe was some prepared and ready-phrased decision—some decision from which the conversation had drifted. "The need of my life is discipline, the habit of persistence, of ignoring side issues and wandering thoughts. Discipline!"

"And work."

"Work, if you like to put it so; it's the same thing. The trouble so far has been I haven't worked hard enough. I've stopped to speak to the woman by the wayside. I've paltered with compromise, and the other thing has caught me. . . . I've got to renounce it, that is all."

"It isn't that your work is contemptible."

"By Jove! No. It's—arduous. It has its dusty moments. There are places to climb that are not only steep but muddy——"

"The world wants leaders. It gives a man of your class a great deal. Leisure. Honor. Training and high traditions——"

"And it expects something back. I know. I am wrong—have been wrong anyhow. This dream has taken me wonderfully. And I must renounce it. After all it is not so much—to renounce a dream. It's no more than deciding to live. There are big things in the world for men to do."

Melville produced an elaborate conceit. "If there is no Venus Anadyomene," he said, "there is Michael and his Sword."

"The stern angel in armor! But then he had a good palpable dragon to slash and not his own desires. And our way nowadays is to do a deal with the dragons somehow, raise the minimum wage and get a better housing for the working classes by hook or by crook."

Melville does not think that was a fair treatment of his suggestion.

"No," said Chatteris, "I've no doubt about the choice. I'm going to fall in—with the species; I'm going to take my place in the ranks in that great battle for the future which is the meaning of life. I want a moral cold bath and I mean to take one. This lax dalliance with dreams and desires must end. I will make a time table for my hours and a rule for my life, I will entangle my honor in controversies, I will give myself to service, as a man should do. Clean-handed work, struggle, and performance."

"And there is Miss Glendower, you know."

"Rather!" said Chatteris, with a faint touch of insincerity. "Tall and straight-eyed and capable. By Jove! if there's to be no Venus Anadyomene, at any rate there will be a Pallas Athene. It is she who plays the reconciler."

And then he said these words: "It won't be so bad, you know."

Melville restrained a movement of impatience, he tells me, at that.

Then Chatteris, he says, broke into a sort of speech. "The case is tried," he said, "the judgment has been given. I am that I am. I've been through it all and worked it out. I am a man and I must go a man's way. There is Desire, the light and guide of the world, a beacon on a headland blazing out. Let it burn! Let it burn! The road runs near it and by it—and past. . . . I've made my choice. I've got to be a man, I've got to live a man and die a man and carry the burden of my class and time. There it is! I've had the dream, but you see I keep hold of reason. Here, with the flame burning, I renounce it. I make my choice. . . . Renunciation! Always—renunciation! That is life for all of us. We have desires, only to deny them, senses that we all must starve. We can live only as a part of ourselves. Why should *I* be exempt. For me, she is evil. For me she is death. . . . Only why have I seen her face? Why have I heard her voice? . . ."

VI

They walked out of the shadows and up a long sloping path until Sandgate, as a little line of lights, came into view below. Presently they came out upon the brow and walked together (the band playing with a remote and sweetening indistinctness far away behind them) towards the cliff at the end. They stood for a little while in silence looking down. Melville made a guess at his companion's thoughts.

"Why not come down to-night?" he asked.

"On a night like this!" Chatteris turned about suddenly and regarded the moonlight and the sea. He stood quite still for a space, and that cold white radiance gave an illusory strength and decision to his face. "No," he said at last, and the word was almost a sigh.

"Go down to the girl below there. End the thing. She will be there, thinking of you——"

"No," said Chatteris, "no."

"It's not ten yet," Melville tried again.

Chatteris thought. "No," he answered, "not to-night. To-morrow, in the light of everyday.

"I want a good, gray, honest day," he said, "with a south-west wind. . . . These still, soft nights! How can you expect me to do anything of that sort to-night?"

And then he murmured as if he found the word a satisfying word to repeat, "Renunciation."

"By Jove!" he said with the most astonishing transition, "but this is a night out of fairyland! Look at the lights of those windows below there and then up—up into this enormous blue of sky. And there, as if it were fainting with moonlight—shines one star."

MOONSHINE TRIUMPHANT

1

J ust precisely what happened after that has been the most impossible thing to disinter. I have given all the things that Melville remembered were said, I have linked them into a conversation and checked them by my cousin's afterthoughts, and finally I have read the whole thing over to him. It is of course no verbatim rendering, but it is, he says, closely after the manner of their talk, the gist was that, and things of that sort were said. And when he left Chatteris, he fully believed that the final and conclusive thing was said. And then he says it came into his head that, apart from and outside this settlement, there still remained a tangible reality, capable of action, the Sea Lady. What was she going to do? The thought toppled him back into a web of perplexities again. It carried him back into a state of inconclusive interrogation past Lummidge's Hotel.

The two men had gone back to the Métropole and had parted with a firm handclasp outside the glare of the big doorway. Chatteris went straight in, Melville fancies, but he is not sure. I understand Melville had some private thinking to do on his own account, and I conceive him walking away in a state of profound preoccupation. Afterwards the fact that the Sea Lady was not to be abolished by renunciations, cropped up in his mind, and he passed back along the Leas, as I have said. His inconclusive interrogations elicited at the utmost that Lummidge's Private and Family Hotel is singularly like any other hotel of its class. Its windows tell no secrets. And there Melville's narrative ends.

With that my circumstantial record necessarily comes to an end also. There are sources, of course, and glimpses. Parker refuses, unhappily—as I explained. The chief of these sources are, first, Gooch, the valet employed by Chatteris; and, secondly, the hall-porter of Lummidge's Private and Family Hotel.

The valet's evidence is precise, but has an air of being irrelevant. He witnesses that at a quarter past eleven he went up to ask Chatteris if there was anything more to do that night, and found him seated in an arm-chair before the open window, with his chin upon his hands, staring at nothing—which, indeed, as Schopenhauer observes in his crowning passage, is the whole of human life.

"More to do?" said Chatteris.

"Yessir," said the valet.

"Nothing," said Chatteris, "absolutely nothing." And the valet, finding this answer quite satisfactory, wished him good-night and departed.

Probably Chatteris remained in this attitude for a considerable time—half an hour, perhaps, or more. Slowly, it would seem, his mood underwent a change. At some definite moment it must have been that his lethargic meditation gave way to a strange activity, to a sort of hysterical reaction against all his resolves and renunciations. His first action seems to me grotesque—and grotesquely pathetic. He went into his dressing-room, and in the morning "his clo'es," said the valet, "was shied about as though 'e'd lost a ticket." This poor worshipper of beauty and the dream shaved! He shaved and washed and he brushed his hair, and, his valet testifies, one of the brushes got "shied" behind the bed. Even this throwing about of brushes seems to me to have done little or nothing to palliate his poor human preoccupation with the toilette. He changed his gray flannels—which suited him very well—for his white ones, which suited him extremely. He must deliberately and conscientiously have made himself quite "lovely," as a schoolgirl would have put it.

And having capped his great "renunciation" by these proceedings, he seems to have gone straight to Lummidge's Private and Family Hotel and demanded to see the Sea Lady.

She had retired.

This came from Parker, and was delivered in a chilling manner by the hall-porter.

Chatteris swore at the hall-porter. "Tell her I'm here," he said.

"She's retired," said the hall-porter with official severity.

"Will you tell her I'm here?" said Chatteris, suddenly white.

"What name, sir?" said the hall-porter, in order, as he explains, "to avoid a frackass."

"Chatteris. Tell her I must see her now. Do you hear, *now?*"

The hall-porter went to Parker, and came half-way back. He wished to goodness he was not a hall-porter. The manager had gone out—it was a stagnant hour. He decided to try Parker again; he raised his voice.

The Sea Lady called to Parker from the inner room. There was an interval of tension.

I gather that the Sea Lady put on a loose wrap, and the faithful Parker either carried her or sufficiently helped her from her bedroom to the couch in the little sitting-room. In the meanwhile the hall-porter hovered on the stairs, praying for the manager—prayers that went unanswered—and Chatteris fumed below. Then we have a glimpse of the Sea Lady.

"I see her just in the crack of the door," said the porter, "as that maid of hers opened it. She was raised up on her hands, and turned so towards the door. Looking exactly like this——"

And the hall-porter, who has an Irish type of face, a short nose, long upper lip, and all the rest of it, and who has also neglected his dentist, projected his face suddenly, opened his eyes very wide, and slowly curved his mouth into a fixed smile, and so remained until he judged the effect on me was complete.

Parker, a little flushed, but resolutely flattening everything to the quality of the commonplace, emerged upon him suddenly. Miss Waters could see Mr. Chatteris for a few minutes. She was emphatic with the "Miss Waters," the more emphatic for all the insurgent stress of the goddess, protestingly emphatic. And Chatteris went up, white and resolved, to that smiling expectant presence. No one witnessed their meeting but Parker—assuredly Parker could not resist seeing that, but Parker is silent—Parker preserves a silence that rubies could not break.

All I know, is this much from the porter:

"When I said she was up there and would see him," he says, "the way he rooshed up was outrageous. This is a Private Family Hotel. Of course one sees things at times even here, but——

"I couldn't find the manager to tell 'im," said the hall-porter. "And what was *I* authorized to do?

"For a bit they talked with the door open, and then it was shut. That maid of hers did it—I lay."

I asked an ignoble question.

"Couldn't ketch a word," said the hall-porter. "Dropped to whispers—instanter."

11

And afterwards—

It was within ten minutes of one that Parker, conferring an amount of decorum on the request beyond the power of any other living being, descended to demand—of all conceivable things—the bath chair!

"I got it," said the hall-porter with inimitable profundity.

And then, having let me realize the fulness of that, he said: "They never used it!"

"No?"

"No! He carried her down in his arms."

"And out?"

"And out!"

He was difficult to follow in his description of the Sea Lady. She wore her wrap, it seems, and she was "like a statue"—whatever he may have meant by that. Certainly not that she was impassive. "Only," said the porter, "she was alive. One arm was bare, I know, and her hair was down, a tossing mass of gold.

"He looked, you know, like a man who's screwed himself up.

"She had one hand holding his hair—yes, holding his hair, with her fingers in among it. . . .

"And when she see my face she threw her head back laughing at me."

"As much as to say, '*got* 'im!'"

"Laughed at me, she did. Bubblin' over."

I stood for a moment conceiving this extraordinary picture. Then a question occurred to me.

"Did *he* laugh?" I asked.

"Gord bless you, sir, laugh? *No!*"

III

The definite story ends in the warm light outside Lummidge's Private and Family Hotel. One sees that bright solitude of the Leas stretching white and blank—deserted as only a seaside front in the small hours can be deserted—and all its electric light ablaze. And then the dark line of the edge where the cliff drops down to the undercliff and sea. And beyond, moonlit, the Channel and its incessant ships. Outside the front of the hotel, which is one of a great array of pallid white façades, stands this little black figure of a hall-porter, staring stupidly into the warm and luminous mystery of the night that has swallowed Sea Lady and Chatteris together. And he is the sole living thing in the picture.

There is a little shelter set in the brow of the Leas, wherein, during the winter season, a string band plays. Close by there are steps that go down precipitously to the lower road below. Down these it must have been they went together, hastening downward out of this life of ours to unknown and inconceivable things. So it is I seem to see them, and surely though he was not in a laughing mood, there was now no doubt nor resignation in his face. Assuredly now he had found himself, for a time at least he was sure of himself, and that at least cannot be misery, though it lead straight through a few swift strides to death.

They went down through the soft moonlight, tall and white and splendid, interlocked, with his arms about her, his brow to her white shoulder and her hair about his face. And she, I suppose, smiled above him and caressed him and whispered to him. For a moment they must have glowed under the warm light of the lamp that is half-way down the steps there, and then the shadows closed about them. He must have crossed the road with her, through the laced moonlight of the tree shadows, and through the shrubs and bushes of the undercliff, into the shadeless moon glare of the beach. There was no one to see that last descent, to tell whether for a moment he looked back before he waded into the phosphorescence, and for a little swam with her, and presently swam no longer, and so was no more to be seen by any one in this gray world of men.

Did he look back, I wonder? They swam together for a little while, the man and the sea goddess who had come for him, with the sky above them and the water about them all, warmly filled with the moonlight and set with shining stars. It was no time for him to think of truth, nor of the honest duties he had left behind him, as they swam together into the unknown. And of the end I can only guess and dream. Did there come a sudden horror upon him at the last, a sudden perception of infinite error, and was he drawn down, swiftly and terribly, a bubbling repentance, into those unknown deeps? Or was she tender and wonderful to the last, and did she wrap her arms about him and draw him down, down until the soft waters closed above him into a gentle ecstasy of death?

Into these things we cannot pry or follow, and on the margin of the softly breathing water the story of Chatteris must end. For the tailpiece to that, let us put that policeman who in the small hours before dawn came upon the wrap the Sea Lady had been wearing just as the tide overtook it. It was not the sort of garment low people sometimes throw away—it was a soft and costly wrap. I seem to see him perplexed and dubious, wrap in charge over his arm and lantern in hand, scanning first the white beach and black bushes behind him and then staring out to sea. It was the inexplicable abandonment of a thoroughly comfortable and desirable thing.

"What were people up to?" one figures him asking, this simple citizen of a plain and observed world. "What do such things mean?

"To throw away such an excellent wrap. . . !"

In all the southward heaven there were only a planet and the sinking moon, and from his feet a path of quivering light must have started and run up to the extreme dark edge before him of the sky. Ever and again the darkness east and west of that glory would be lit by a momentary gleam of phosphorescence; and far out the lights of ships were shining bright and yellow. Across its shimmer a black fishing smack was gliding out of mystery into mystery. Dungeness shone from the west a pin-point of red light, and in the east the tireless glare of that great beacon on Gris-nez wheeled athwart the sky and vanished and came again.

I picture the interrogation of his lantern going out for a little way, a stain of faint pink curiosity upon the mysterious vast serenity of night.

H. G. WELLS (1866–1946) was an English writer well known for his science fiction. His oeuvre includes novels such as *The Time Machine* and *The War of the Worlds*, as well as short stories and nonfiction works of social commentary, history, satire, and biography.

JIM TIERNEY grew up in the rural farmlands of southeastern Pennsylvania. He studied illustration at the University of the Arts in Philadelphia, where he met his wife and frequent collaborator Sara Wood. They spent a decade designing book covers in New York before leaving the city to build a studio in the attic of Jim's childhood home, where they currently work and live with their family.